Wildcat Under Glass

Wildcat Under Glass

by ALKI ZEI

TRANSLATED FROM THE GREEK

by EDWARD FENTON

HOLT, RINEHART AND WINSTON

New York   Chicago   San Francisco

Published simultaneously in Canada by Holt, Rinehart and
Winston of Canada, Limited.
Library of Congress Catalog Card Number: 68-11835
Printed in the United States of America

SBN: 03–068010–7
Published, May, 1968
Second Printing, March, 1969

This translation is dedicated to
Thea Deppy
for many reasons,
some of which she already knows.

About Greece and Freedom

▣ Ancient Greece's name and history are known throughout the civilized world because at one time Greece was the center of world culture. Science, philosophy and art had been developed there to an extraordinary degree.

The history of modern Greece, however, is not well known to most of us. It is equally absorbing—not because of its encouragement of the arts and sciences, but because it demonstrates the thirst and struggle for freedom and true human dignity.

In 1453, with the fall of Constantinople, the Turks conquered all of Greece. The Greeks lived for four hundred years in slavery. It is characteristic that, throughout this long period, when only a few so-called schools existed in the entire land, when everything was uncertain, including life itself, the Greeks lost neither their religion, nor their language nor their national identity. Nor did they lose their thirst for liberty.

The struggle for freedom from the Turks began in 1821. It lasted nearly ten years. It cost much Greek blood. But once again the name of Greece took its place on the map of Europe.

The first ruler of the reborn nation was a Greek, John Capodistrias. After his assassination, the great powers, France, Britain and Russia, decided to give Greece a king—one who was not, however, a Greek. The first was Otto of Bavaria. He loved Greece but never really understood the country he ruled. He first set foot on Greek soil in 1833 and fled into exile in 1862. After this, the powers chose George, of the Danish dynasty of Glücksburg. This family has ruled until today.

From 1821 until now, the road that Greece had to travel was long and difficult. But much was accomplished.

In the first World War, Greece fought on the side of the Allies. During it, and until 1935, Eleutherios Venizelos played an important role in the country's history. He was a great political figure who believed in the democratic ideal.

In 1936, George II, the uncle of the present King Constantine, was king. At the same time Adolf Hitler, in Germany, and Benito Mussolini, in Italy, entrenched their fascist governments. They were also helping their fellow-fascist, General Franco, establish his regime in Spain, where a savage civil war was taking place. Many foreigners from all over the world fought with the Spaniards against Franco and against fascism. Among them were Greeks.

And then, in 1936, fascism reached Greece with General John Metaxas who took over the government and established his dictatorship. The prisons and the desert islands of Greece were filled with those who did not support him and who resisted his regime. Many of these, intellectuals and politicians as well as ordinary citizens, never returned to their homes. They died in prison and in exile.

Metaxas knew perfectly well that his regime could never be a firm one unless the people believed in it. Dictatorship is something which is alien and strange to Greece, the country where the idea of democracy was born. Something had to be changed: the thinking of the young people. The children would have to be taught to love something which their parents and their ancestors had detested: They would have to learn to believe in values which ignored the basic human rights. And so he founded the National Youth Organization. Fortunately, this system of indoctrination did not endure for long. Metaxas died at the beginning of World War II. And the war itself disrupted everything.

Once again the Greeks fought for freedom and for the rights of man. They gave the Allies their first victory, and fought bitterly beside them for four long years so that man could still walk in freedom and in pride.

Edward Fenton

⊒ Contents ⊒

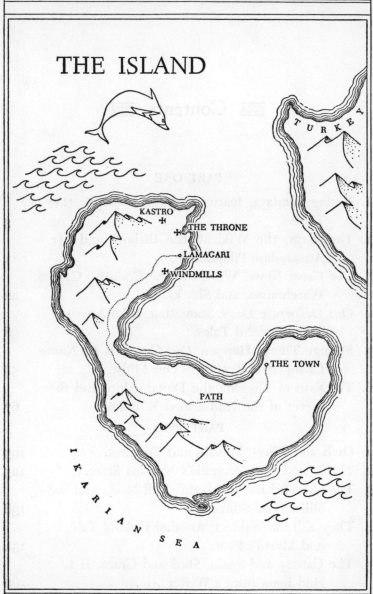

THE ISLAND

TURKEY

KASTRO ✠

✠ THE THRONE

○ LAMAGARI

✠ WINDMILLS

○ THE TOWN

PATH

IKARIAN SEA

THE TOWN

SEA WALL

ALEXIS'S HOUSE

TOWN
SQUARE

GREAT-AUNT DESPINA'S HOUSE

MRS. ANGELIKI'S

SCHOOL

LAMAGARI

WAREHOUSES

PIPITSA'S
CASTLE

GRANDFATHER'S
CASTLE

SHACKS

SEA WALL

ANTONI'S
BOAT

Part One

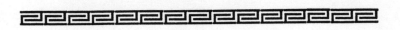

Part One

⊒ 1 ⊒

Boring Sundays, Icarus, and
the Multiplication Tables.

⊒ Sunday, in winter, is the dreariest day of the week. I would like to know if all the children in the world have such a boring time as my sister Myrto and I do, especially in the afternoon when it starts to get dark early and we have to stay indoors and we don't know what to do with ourselves. Ever since morning we had been playing and quarreling and making up. We had been reading, too: I, *David Copperfield*, and Myrto, something by Jack London. And there was nothing, absolutely nothing, left to do.

Papa and Mama were playing cards, as they did every Sunday evening, at Mr. Pericles' house. He is the director of Papa's bank. Great-aunt Despina, our grandfather's sister, had gone off to pay calls on her lady friends. Stamatina, the maid, had her day off. And so, as on most Sunday evenings, we were left alone with our grandfather. When the weather was fair, Grandfather usually took us

3

for a walk, and then, as soon as it got dark, we would return home. That was when the great dreariness would set in. Grandfather would lock himself in his study with his Ancients. That's what Myrto and I call Grandfather's books, because they are all in ancient Greek, which is not the same thing at all as the modern Greek we speak.

We wandered out to the glass-enclosed porch and looked at the sea. A gale was blowing, and the waves broke on the rocks and sprayed the windows, leaving drops that trickled down the panes. They looked just like tears. So we made up the saddest stories we could think of, such as "Papa's Death," and "Our New Stepfather Who Is Even Crueler Than David Copperfield's."

Then we pretended that our grandfather was a poor beggar and we were dressed in rags and had to go around with him in the cold begging for bread from door to door.

But on that particular Sunday we were so bored that Myrto said that "Our Grandfather the Beggar Man" was the silliest story we had ever made up. We sat around for a while, sulking. After that, each of us chose a pane of glass and we said that whoever's pane had the most drops fall on it would win. And since I was the one who always won, Myrto said that it was the stupidest game we had ever played.

So I said, "Why don't we make up a story about the wildcat?"

I hadn't even finished the sentence before I was sorry I'd said anything. I froze.

"Aren't you ashamed, Melia? That's all I can say!"

4

Myrto snapped. "You're so conceited, you think you can even make up stories about the wildcat!"

Perhaps she was right. Because when it comes to the wildcat, which is stuffed and stands in a glass case in the big parlor, the only one who can tell stories about it is our cousin Niko. Niko lives in Athens and he is studying chemistry at the University. Every summer he comes to the island on which we live and goes to the country with us. He tells us all about the wildcat's adventures. He doesn't tell them only to us, but also to the other children that we know out in the country.

Of course Great-aunt Despina likes to tell how her husband killed the wildcat, when it kept swimming over from the coast of Turkey to kill sheep on the island. But that is a story for grown-ups and none of us children believe it. But Niko knows a marvelous tale about the wildcat in the case, a story that goes on and on without ever ending, and every summer he picks it up where he left off the year before.

It had grown dark, so dark that it was impossible to make out the sea, not even the waves. We could only hear a loud "paff!" and the panes would suddenly be covered with tears again. The street outside was deserted. Then I started imagining that our island was empty, that all the people had left the town and the villages and had gone somewhere far away, and the only thing that had stayed behind was our glassed-in porch with the two of us, sailing through the foamy sea.

"Aren't you ashamed!" Myrto repeated.

I realized that she had said it just to have an excuse for

us to start speaking again, even if it was only to quarrel. And I was looking for an excuse to creep closer to her because it was very dark and I was afraid. It was then that we heard the chanting of the magic words: "Pa, vou, ga, de, ke, zo, ni. . . ."

It was our grandfather. Whenever he finished reading he would intone the syllables of a strange language called Byzantine. Whenever Myrto and I wanted to show off in front of other children we would gabble between us in what would appear to be a foreign language. One of us would say, "Pa, vou, ga," and the other would answer, "De, ke, zo, ni." Then they would ask, "But what language are you talking?" And we would look down our noses and answer, "Don't you understand? It's Byzantine."

Our grandfather came out to the porch and led us into the dining room. He cracked walnuts and gave them to us, with honey, to eat. When Myrto asked to have her little dish filled for the third time, Grandfather said, "Myrto, which would you rather have: more walnuts, or to hear me tell a myth?"

"More walnuts, of course," she answered. "Since you can't eat myths."

What a strange man our grandfather is! He isn't at all like the other children's grandfathers. He is very tall, like a cypress tree; and he walks without a cane. His back isn't a bit bent. Everyone on the island calls him "The Sage."

He knows all of Homer's *Iliad* and *Odyssey* by heart. He never tells us fairy stories about dragons and princes: only myths about the ancient Greek gods, and legends of the old heroes. Sometimes I believe that my grandfather must really be an ancient Greek. But I never dare mention this, not even to Myrto, because her only answer would be, "Stuff and nonsense!"

"Well, what do you want to do now?" Grandfather asked, since we had eaten all the walnuts.

We didn't say anything, because if we said that we wanted him to play Lotto with us he would only reply, "Let me tell you a myth instead. You can always play Lotto with Stamatina."

"Well, then, I'll tell you a myth," Grandfather said, and began the story of Daedalus and Icarus.

". . . And so Icarus," he concluded, "with the wings that his father Daedalus had made for him, began to fly like a bird. But he flew so high, almost as high as the sun, that the wax which held his wings together began to melt. And that is how he fell into the sea and was drowned. And the sea into which he fell is called the Icarian Sea. . . ."

And right there, in the Icarian Sea, lies our island. Even though it is one of the largest of the Greek islands, with towns and villages scattered over it, it looks no bigger than a little dot on the globe. Beyond it are the other islands, and after that, the mainland of Greece, and then the neighboring countries.

What a lovely thing it would be to put two wings on your back and fly! Supposing it were a dreary Sunday. You could say, "I'll just stick my wings on and fly off for a minute to Japan or China or to Africa, to see if the Japanese children and the Chinese children and the African children are as bored on Sundays as I am." And I'd find

7

out if they too play hopscotch and jacks and jump-rope.

"Do you really think, Grandfather, that man will ever be able to put on wings and fly?" I asked.

"Stuff and nonsense!" Myrto exclaimed before he could reply. But Grandfather did not let her go on.

He said, "Even that might happen in fifty or maybe a hundred years. It is now January, 1936. By January in 1986 men might even be able to fly, like Icarus, close to the sun without melting their wings."

"Ooooooooh, and what are we supposed to do until then?" Myrto said. "By that time we'll have turned into old ladies so we won't be able to fly."

Grandfather chided her for being so selfish. "If everybody else thought the same way," he said, "no one would ever have discovered anything in the world. The scientists would say, 'Why should we wear ourselves out to discover this or that, since by the time our inventions are perfected we'll either be old or dead?'

"But the scientists, my dear Miss Myrto," Grandfather went on, "think about humanity and not just about themselves. Even though they may no longer be alive, their names remain immortal."

"I think I would like to be an inventor," said Myrto.

"If all the inventors knew their multiplication tables as badly as you do," Grandfather told her, "nothing in the world would ever have gotten invented."

We never dreamed that particular Sunday would end so badly. Grandfather started asking Myrto the seven times seven, and she—you'd think she did it on purpose—got everything all mixed up. In fact, she said that seven times eight make forty-six, while Grandfather maintained that it was fifty-six. And she insisted that it was forty-six until Grandfather grew angry.

"If you don't learn your multiplication tables by heart, backwards and forwards, you'll never go to a proper school," he said, and sent us off to bed.

We didn't go to school. Grandfather gave us lessons at home. Every year we took examinations as "Instructees at Home," and got promoted. They didn't want to send us to a public school because, as Grandfather said, there were so many children in each classroom that a whole term could pass without your ever having been called on to recite. In our neighborhood there was also Mr. Karanasis' private school. But Papa said it "didn't fit our purse."

When we were in our beds and ready for sleep, Myrto started saying it was all my fault that Grandfather had scolded her about the multiplication tables, because I was the one who had asked if man would ever really be able to fly. How was I to know that in order to be able to fly you had to know the multiplication tables by heart, backwards and forwards, and that then Grandfather would start asking Myrto to recite them and get angry?

Was it possible that everything would ever go well on Sundays? If we went to school, we'd like Sunday because it would mean we could stay home. But now——

"Oh, if we could only go to school!" I said aloud. But Myrto had the blankets right up over her head and pretended that she couldn't hear. So then, louder, I said, "Ev-po? Li-po?"

"Li-po, li-po," she answered stubbornly from under the blankets.

That wasn't Byzantine. It was a language we had made

up, that only the two of us could understand. "Ev-po" meant very happy. "Li-po" meant very sad. And if one of us didn't ask the other every night, we couldn't sleep. I don't know why, but on Sundays, practically every time, we answered, "Li-po. Li-po."

If I had wings now, like Icarus, I would be able to fly from country to country and ask all the children of the whole world, "Ev-po? Li-po?"

⧉ 2 ⧉
Thursdays, the Wildcat, the Bishop, and Mr. Amstradam Pikipikiram.

⧉ If Sundays were the most boring days, then Thursdays were the most fun. That was because Great-aunt Despina was at home to callers every Thursday. The big parlor, which had remained shut up all the rest of the week with nobody daring to set foot in it, was opened then. And so, on Thursdays we were able to see the wildcat that stood, stuffed, in its glass case in the middle of the room.

When we were small, Great-aunt Despina used to threaten us. "Just you break anything, and I'll put you in the glass case with the wildcat!" We were little then, and easily frightened. But now, even when we implored her to unlock the case she wouldn't do it.

The reason we wanted her to unlock the case was so we could touch the wildcat and see its eyes close up. Its eyes were very strange. One of them was black, and the other was blue, sky-blue!

Great-aunt Despina always maintained that the wild-cat's eyes were glass, and that the taxidermist made a mistake and gave it beads that didn't match. That's what she said because she didn't know the marvelous story that Niko had told us.

"Once upon a time there lived in the forest a wild-cat (the very same one that's under glass now) and it had one black eye and one that was all blue. It was born like that. One day it would keep the sky-blue eye open while the black one slept. And the next day it would see out of its black eye while the blue one stayed shut.

"When it saw out of its blue eye it was tame, like a cat. It walked among men and helped them, and played with the children and with the small animals of the forest. But when its black eye was open it destroyed the work of man, and the little animals ran and hid in their burrows when they heard him pass."

Stamatina had promised us that when the time came for the general house-cleaning before we left for the country, she would manage to get the key of the glass case from Great-aunt Despina so that she could give it a thorough dusting, and then she would let us see the wildcat up close. We'd have plenty to tell the children in the country, then, about how we'd touched it with our own hands, and how we'd been able to see if its eyes were glass, or real.

It was fourteen whole days since we had laid eyes on the wildcat. I had been sick the Thursday before, and so we hadn't gone downstairs to the parlor when Great-aunt Despina's callers came.

As soon as we awoke that morning I knew at once that it was Thursday, because Myrto asked, "Can't you remind me of something cute that I did?"

Myrto is Great-aunt Despina's "pride and joy." That's what Niko calls her when he teases her. Every Thursday Great-aunt Despina summons us and we have to go downstairs when her visitors arrive. Then she makes Myrto recount her "cute deeds." (That's what we call them.)

"Well, can't you remind me of a single cute deed?" Myrto insisted.

"Why don't you tell them about the time when you were four years old and you asked the Bishop if he ever wet himself when he was little?" I said.

"Are you crazy? The Bishop will be there today!"

"Then tell them what you said to Grandfather on Sunday when he asked you if you wanted him to give you more walnuts or tell you a myth, and you said, 'Walnuts, of course. You can't eat myths.'"

"Is that supposed to be a cute deed?" Myrto wondered.

"I think it is," I said, "because I heard Grandfather telling Great-aunt Despina, and she said 'How cute!'"

"All right," Myrto agreed. "But it's not enough."

"I know!" I cried. "Remember when Papa broke his leg and you asked him, 'If you die, Papa, where will we find money for food?'"

"Thanks a lot, Melissa, for reminding me," Myrto said in a very sarcastic voice.

I guess I forgot to mention that my real name is Melissa. Maybe it's because I'm a little ashamed of it. Melia is what everyone calls me. Grandfather wanted me to be named Melissa because it was my grandmother's name. There is a photograph album in the house, and in one of the pictures there is a baby with a head like a bean, and underneath it is written, "Queen Melissa." And I'm that baby!

Grandfather says that Melissa was an ancient queen. But it seems that nobody except Grandfather knows that. What everybody does know is that Melissa means "bee" in Greek. As soon as I say my name is Melissa, they all, big and small, ask me, "And have you any honey?"

Mama came into our room. When she saw us still in our nightgowns she began to scold.

"Your grandfather is waiting to give you a lesson, and you're still traipsing around in your nightgowns. If you don't get to your lessons on time you'll never learn anything."

"As though we didn't *want* to go!" Myrto muttered to me while we were hastily washing.

We ran downstairs to our grandfather, who was waiting; and Myrto kept saying the 7 times 7 under her breath. She tangled her foot and went tumbling down the stairs.

"You see how right Grandfather is!" I called after her. "You've barely managed to learn the multiplication tables properly, and you're already flying!"

"Stuff and nonsense!" she answered furiously. "Look at yourself. You don't even know how many stamens an apple blossom has!"

"But you're two grades ahead of me, that's why you know—"

It was a good thing Grandfather called out to me, because otherwise it would have grown into a real fight.

That's the way Myrto was. As soon as she learned anything new, she had to crow about it all over the place. In fact, from the moment she learned about botany, she never left anyone in peace.

In the afternoon we were sitting in our room waiting for Stamatina to call us to go down to the parlor.

Stamatina charged in. She was in a temper.

"Why does she send me," she raged, "since she knows he refuses to come every time?"

Every Thursday Great-aunt Despina sent Stamatina to tell Grandfather to come down to the parlor to her visitors. And every time, Grandfather failed to come.

"And she sends me again, today of all days," Stamatina went on, "when the billy goat will be there. Your grandfather can't stand the sight of him."

"What billy goat?" we demanded at once.

"The Bishop," Stamatina said. At once she cast us a stern glance. "Now just be sure and let your aunt know that I called him that!"

At that Myrto got properly angry.

"You know perfectly well that we never repeat things."

"All right, all right," laughed Stamatina. "I just thought I'd mention it."

"And you don't even know how many stamens the apple blossom has! Or the pear blossom!" Myrto went on in a superior tone to show her annoyance.

Stamatina didn't answer. I wondered how Myrto could say such a thing when she knows that poor Stamatina doesn't even know how to write her own name.

After that she unbraided Myrto's pigtail and started combing it out. Myrto had blond hair and green eyes. She was really very pretty. Everybody said so. She looked like Great-aunt Despina when she was a girl. That was why she was Great-aunt Despina's pet. And when Great-aunt Despina died, the house we lived in, which belonged to her, was going to be left to Myrto. I had black curly hair and took after Papa. But he didn't have anything to leave me, except for his briefcase, which was leather and had the design of a gazelle on it. Turning her head, Myrto said to me, "We will always live together, Melia. After all, what would I do, all by myself, in such an enormous house?"

"Just think!" I told her. "The house will be all ours. We'll unlock the case when the wildcat's blue eye is open and we'll let him walk around anywhere he wants!"

Then we went down to the parlor. It was full of people. The Bishop sat with three ladies and they were playing cards. Great-aunt Despina nodded to us to go over and kiss his hand. We waited a little because he was dealing. Then he gave us his hand to kiss without even glancing at us. His hand was soft and limp, like a slice of bread.

After that we crept very quickly behind the glass case, and this time nobody remembered to ask Myrto to recount any of her cute deeds. They were all talking at once. In fact, they were shouting so loudly that, for a moment, we thought the wildcat opened his black eye to glare savagely at them.

It was queer, staring at the visitors through the panes

16

of the case. The Mayor, who was short and thin, seemed at one instant to have grown terribly tall, and the next instant he was short and dumpy.

He said that the nation was in danger and that only the King could save it. Then he said that the Bolsheviks were coming. They would snatch us children from our parents and they would hang the Bishop in the middle of the town square!

The Mayor's wife always wore white kid gloves up to her elbows. She never took them off, not even to drink her coffee. She waved her hands and cried out in a high singsong voice, "How friiiiiightful! How friiiiiiightful!"

"Look," I said to Myrto. "From this corner, through the glass, her hands look just like branches."

Myrto squeezed herself in beside me to look. Just then someone spoke in such a loud voice that the glass case shook and it seemed to us as though the wildcat leaped from its stand. It was Mr. Amstradam Pikipikiram. That wasn't really his name, but it was what we had christened him. He was the Dutch Consul on our island, and every phrase he uttered was invariably prefixed by, "Well, as a matter of fact, in Amsterdam——", even though he had never been there, not even once.

Amsterdam may be the biggest city in Holland, but it only reminded us of the old nonsense rhyme that we children used for counting out when we played hide and seek:

> Am-stra-dam, piki-piki-ram,
> pourri-pourri-pa,
> Am-stra-dam!

"A dictator, a Hitler! That's what Greece needs!" Mr. Amstradam Pikipikiram shouted again.

Then we heard Mama's voice. "Oh, surely not a Hitler!"

Papa made a sign to Mama not to say any more, and Great-aunt Despina began handing out the coffee and cake. We emerged from behind the glass case to see if she was serving the cake on the dishes which were hand-painted with exotic, many-colored birds. But as soon as Papa saw us he told us to go upstairs to our room. I caught a glimpse of his hands, and they were trembling as though he were terribly angry.

We didn't go to our room. Instead, we ran straight to our grandfather.

Grandfather was standing on the top step of the little ladder that he keeps to reach the top shelves of his bookcase. He was leafing through one of his Ancients.

"Grandfather, they're going to hang the Bishop in the middle of the town square!" Myrto announced. "And when the wind rises, his robe will billow out, just like a big black sail!"

"Grandfather," I announced in my turn, "they're going to take us children away from you, too, and maybe they'll throw us in a big——"

Grandfather did not let me finish. He slammed his Ancient shut.

"What foolishness are you talking?"

"It's not what we say. It's what the Mayor says," Myrto told him. "He said that's what's going to happen when the Bolsheviks come."

Then Grandfather got very angry indeed. We had

never seen him so angry before. He climbed down from the ladder and went up to us. Then he said very solemnly, "All that is foolishness, even if the Mayor says it. Having a king isn't enough for them. They want even worse!"

"What do you mean, 'worse,' Grandfather?"

"A dictatorship is worse than a king."

We looked blankly at him. Then Grandfather started talking about the ancient Greeks who had a leader whose name was Pericles, just like the director of Papa's bank, and they had a democracy, and everyone was happy and they all lived harmoniously together. And that was called the Golden Age of Pericles. And we too had a democracy like that, but now we had a king. But the worst thing of all is a dictatorship.

"Why?"

"Because," Grandfather said, "a dictatorship ignores the will of the people. It takes away their freedom, and without that freedom there is no more harmony."

He would have told us more, but we were sleepy and started yawning, so he broke off and said, "Now run off to bed, and sweet dreams!"

While we were brushing our teeth, Myrto said we ought to wash our mouths with soap because we had kissed the Bishop's hand. Then each of us puffed out her breath at the other, asking, "Do I still smell bishopy?"

When we were curled up in bed Myrto said, "I don't care what Grandfather says about his old Pericles, I love kings. Aunt Despina says that if it hadn't been for King Constantine, Greece would still be a vassal of the Turks."

"What are you talking about?" I said angrily. "Grand-

father says that if it hadn't been for the statesmanship of
our great Prime Minister Venizelos we would still be under Turkish rule."

"No," she insisted, "the King!"

"Niko says that all kings are stupid."

"In fairy stories!"

"No, really."

"Oh, you're too young to understand anything!"

"And you're a sneak, a sneak, a sneak!" I answered in a
fury. "Last year you were all for Venizelos because he
was democratic. You cut out his pictures and stuck them
up on the wall, and you even said you wished he was your
grandfather!"

"Well, so what?" Myrto shouted. "Now I'm for the
King!"

"And you've forgotten," I went on, "how when we were
little and Venizelos came here, to our island, for the
opening of the new post office, Venizelos shook Grandfather's hand and patted our heads. And after that, remember, our hair smelled of Cuticura soap, not bishopy!"

"So what?" Myrto retorted mockingly. "Well, the King
washes with rose water and jasmine cologne and he
wears a gold crown on his head!"

Just then Stamatina came into the room to close the
shutters, and we asked her, "Stamatina, whose side are
you on, Venizelos' or the King's?"

"I'm on my own side," she snapped. "What sort of talk
is this at bedtime?"

She slammed the windows shut. "Whoever comes into
power," she went on, "they're not coming to me for ad-

vice. No matter what happens, I'll still be a servant, unable to read or write."

After Stamatina went away, I thought about how mixed up and absurd everything was.

"Ev-po? Li-po?" Myrto called from her bed.

"Li-po, li-po," I answered stubbornly. Then it was my turn to ask, "Ev-po? Li-po?"

"Ev-po, ev-po!" Myrto sang out.

⊒ 3 ⊒

The Great News. We Go to the Country.
Castles, Warehouses, and Shacks.

⊒ So the days passed and the time approached for us
to leave for the country. We waited impatiently for the
day to come when the parlor would be dusted, so that
Stamatina would open the case and we could see the
wildcat. The hot weather had already set in. The sea was
full of sailboats and motorboats. It wasn't boring any
more, not even when we had to spend a whole Sunday in
the glassed-in porch.

We could watch the boats coming and going, some
with oars, others with unfurled sails. And with our eyes
we could follow the motorboats as they passed each
other, leaving a wake of spray behind them. Of course it
would be different in the country. There, we could get
inside the boats and sit in the prow with our feet dan-
gling in the water. There were still ten days before we
would go there. Every year we left town on the same
date, and I was counting off the days on the calendar
when I heard Mama saying to Great-aunt Despina, "Why

don't you take them and go? Summer has started so early this year."

I jumped for joy and ran to tell Myrto.

"Stuff and nonsense," she said. "Every year we leave on the tenth of June."

"But Mama said that it's hot, and——"

"Stuff and nonsense," she repeated. But she ran off to ask Great-aunt Despina if it was true.

She came back terribly excited and out of breath from running. "I have news for you, news that will make you jump right out of your skin! But it's not what you said. We're going to school!" she shrilled, hopping around on one foot. "To a real school! Papa just came home from work and he said so. Mr. Pericles spoke to Mr. Karanasis, and Mr. Karanasis is going to let us go to his school with a discount."

"What's a discount?" I asked, upset because I didn't know what it meant.

"A discount means we pay less," Myrto explained. "And so it will fit our purse. But you can't go because you don't know how many stamens an apple blossom has."

I knew she was teasing me, but I didn't feel like starting a fight. We went off to find the grown-ups. They were all in the dining room, sitting around the big table. We wanted to ask them about the school, but no one paid any attention to us. Mama had pencil and paper in front of her and was figuring: so much for tuition (with the discount, of course), so much for the educational tax (without discount), so much for uniforms, so much for schoolbags, and a pile of other boring things.

I said in a low voice, "Let's go and tell the wildcat the news."

At first we couldn't make out anything in the parlor because the cherry-colored velvet curtains were drawn. After a while our eyes grew used to the dark and then we were so terrified that we grabbed hold of each other's hands and stood there as though we had been turned into stone. The wildcat had turned around in his case! He no longer stood as he always had, facing the wall. His head was now pointed in the direction of the window, from which he could look out over the sea.

Neither of us said a word to the other. For a moment I thought that perhaps it was only a notion of my own, something that I had imagined. But Myrto gripped my fingers so hard that I understood that she too was scared.

"Did you see that?" I managed to say.

"Yes," she whispered back.

We raced out of the parlor and made for the kitchen, to find Stamatina.

"Did you dust the case?" we cried in one voice.

"What are you shouting about?" she said. "If I had, I'd have told you. But your aunt won't give up the key. She wants to dust it herself."

Of course we had no intention of asking Great-aunt Despina because she would certainly have answered, "Yes, I turned it around."

Whereas if we had asked Niko he would have started to tell us some new tale about the wildcat, some fantastic adventure. Perhaps he would have told us that it had turned around in the window in order to sight the magic ship that was coming to carry it away from the island, the ship that would bear it off to some distant land.

I didn't know what had come over the grown-ups. They were always talking about how black the situation was. Every evening when Papa came home from work, Grandfather would ask him, "Any news?"

"The situation is pretty black," Papa would reply.

"Does it look as though there will be a dictatorship?" Grandfather would ask him.

"It looks very black indeed," Papa would answer.

"The King would never permit it," Great-aunt Despina would assert, breaking into the conversation.

And then the grown-ups would start arguing, worse than us when we were fighting over the raindrops on the boringest Sunday. When we asked Grandfather what "the situation is black" was supposed to mean, he told us that it meant that democracy was dead: not the democracy of the Golden Age of Pericles, but democracy in our own time. Then he quoted an ancient proverb, but it was so ancient we didn't understand a word of it.

And so, when our cat had kittens, one of them dark as coal and the other white, Myrto and I named them Blackie and Democracy. Grandfather burst into laughter when we told him, but Great-aunt Despina looked annoyed.

"It's our fault for saying things in front of the children," she said.

The grown-ups only made everything more confusing to us, which is what nearly always happens anyway. Besides, all we could think of then was Lamagari.

Lamagari was where we went every summer. It was opposite the town, on the other side of the bay. At night, from there, we could see all the lights of the town, and when there was a dead calm we could even hear the sounds of the town, as though from a very long way off. Lamagari wasn't even a village. The only people who lived there were the ones who worked in the warehouses, a number of long narrow buildings where the wine barrels were stored. All the wine that was pressed from grapes that grew in the vineyards all around was kept in them. The people lived in shacks, little low-roofed houses, some of which were built out of mud bricks, and others of stone.

There were also a few two-storied stone houses with verandas and courtyards, and these were called "castles," even ours, which had only three rooms to it. All the people who owned the warehouses spent the summer in these houses. We were the exceptions. We didn't even own a single wine barrel that we could launch in the sea when it got old and sail around in, like a real boat. But we had our castle in Lamagari because once, a long time ago, Grandfather's father owned warehouses, but he sold most of them, along with most of his vineyards, so that Grandfather could study and buy his Ancients.

It was a half-hour's boat ride from the town to reach Lamagari. Every year we waited for Antoni, the boatman, to come and get us with his *Crystal*. That's what his boat was called. It was a strange name for a boat, but it was also the name of his wife who was drowned in the sea. When Antoni came to fetch us he often brought his daughter, Artemis, along with him. She was our best friend in Lamagari.

We always left with Great-aunt Despina and Grandfather. Papa and Mama came only for weekends—fortunately for us because Papa, who wasn't born on an island, was so terrified of the sea that he wouldn't let us go a single step by ourselves. And he thought we were so stupid as to go off and slip on the ancient stone walls and fall right down, head first, into the sea and get drowned.

As for Great-aunt Despina, all she asked was that we didn't track sand into the house and that we washed our feet every night before going to bed. As for the sea, she would say, "It'll do you both good to get some salt baked into your skins." And all that Grandfather demanded of us was that we repeated correctly at night the ancient proverb that he taught us every morning while we had breakfast.

We were already set to leave for Lamagari. The previous night Papa had summoned us and repeated his "Ten Commandments"—which is what Myrto and I called them. He handed them down to us every year and we had learned them by heart.

The Ten Commandments (Papa's)
1. You must not swim in water over your heads.
2. You must not go around barefoot.
3. You must not stay in the water too long.
4. You must not climb trees.
5. You must not eat unripe grapes.
6. You must not eat unwashed grapes.

7. You must not go sailing when there are no grown-ups in the boat.
8. You must not go clambering on the rocks.
9. You must not wander out of range of Great-aunt Despina's voice.
10. You must not fight.

We listened to them and said, "Yes, Papa."

But the instant we set foot on Lamagari, we would forget them all. How could we possibly obey all those mustnots that Papa insisted on? In that case, why bother to go to the country? And so the Ten Commandments were observed only on weekends, when Papa came. Those were what we called our "Desperate Days." When the other children made plans to go to the far-out rocks for limpets and crabs, we would have to tell them, "We can't go. It's the beginning of our Desperate Days."

We sat in the glassed-in porch and waited for Antoni to come and pick us up. The sea was full of boats, but we could pick out the *Crystal* at once.

"There it is!" we yelled. "It's coming!" And we hung out as far as we could to see if Artemis had come with it.

Soon we could make out a tiny red dot darting here and there at Antoni's side. After a while we could hear a faint voice, far off in the sea: "Myrtooooooo! Meeeeeeeelia!"

"Arteeeeeemis!" we shrieked. And then we could distinguish our friend in her red skirt, waving her arms at us.

No sooner had we set foot in the boat than we all began hugging each other.

"Easy, there! You'll capsize the house!" That's what Antoni called his boat: the house. Maybe that was because in summer he even slept in it.

Artemis was a year older than I, and a year younger than Myrto. That way we could each have her for a friend. She had never gone to school, and since Antoni didn't know how to read or write, he couldn't teach her. Even so, Artemis knew lots of things. She knew the name of every fish, even the tiniest. She knew what bait you needed to catch each one. She knew where the rocks were that had limpets on them, and the nearest places for finding crayfish. She could fish all by herself, even for octopus. And if Antoni had let her, she could even have handled a boat with sails.

"How's the wildcat?" Artemis whispered.

Then we told her how the wildcat had turned its face toward the sea, waiting for the magic ship that would carry it away from the island to some faraway country.

On the ancient sea wall, waiting for us, the children were gathered. There were Manoli, Odysseus, and little Aurora, all shouting to us. And the minute we set foot on shore, they pulled out little reed whistles and began blowing them. Great-aunt Despina and Grandfather and Antoni all went on ahead toward the castle with the luggage. We trailed behind with the children.

Stamatina was waiting for us at the castle. She had arrived a day ahead of us to clean the house. We took off our sandals as fast as we could. Myrto kicked off one of hers so violently that it flew through the air and landed on a shelf.

"There go Papa's Ten Commandments!" she said.

We ran below to Grandfather's Vineyard. We called it that because it was Grandfather himself who cultivated it and watered it. He was the only one of all the people who lived in the castles who worked in his vineyard. We couldn't run very fast because those first days, until the soles of our feet got hardened, the stones and thorns hurt. All the same, we didn't want to wear shoes. We wanted to be just like the children from the shacks. We loved them. It didn't matter to us that they spoke in funny accents. In fact, when people stopped us on the road to ask us anything, we would answer in the same country accents, so that they would think we were children from the shacks.

Down in the vineyard the children were waiting for us, enthroned in an enormous almond tree. Grandfather's Vineyard didn't even have a single bunch of grapes in it. It was planted with tomatoes. In the middle of it stood the almond tree.

Niko had made up a whole legend about this vineyard.

Once it was filled with vines that had black grapes on them. But it made the almond tree sad to have all that black around it. Then, one night when the wildcat's black eye was asleep and it was seeing out of its sky-blue one, it came along and uprooted the grapevines and planted cheerful red tomatoes, just to make the almond tree happy.

Myrto and I clambered up into the tree to join the

others, and they all wanted to know about the wildcat. Artemis had already told them how it had turned around in its case in order to look down at the sea.

"And then?" Manoli asked.

"Then what?" we said.

"Oh, if I could only see that wildcat, just once," Manoli sighed, "even if it was inside the case."

But we didn't talk any more about the wildcat. After all, who except for Niko could tell stories about it? And in a few days Niko himself would arrive in Lamagari.

We began to jump up and down. The branches of the almond tree went up and down like swings. Any passer-by would have known right away that Myrto and I weren't from the shacks. The other children were dark-skinned from the sun. Their arms and legs were dusted white from the salt in the water. Artemis' jet-black hair was almost blond at the roots from the sun. But in a few days we too would be black as kettles, and we would talk just like the people in the shacks.

"There she is!" Manoli suddenly shouted. "She's coming!"

We all turned our heads.

It was Pipitsa, another girl from town who also lived in a castle. Pipitsa: could anyone possibly imagine a sillier name? None of us could stand the sight of her. Nearly all the warehouses full of wine barrels belonged to her father, and Pipitsa puffed herself out like a turkey cock whenever she heard the word "warehouses." She was the same age as I, but she didn't even know how to swim. We called her the "Big Pest" because wherever we went her mother insisted that we take her along. And there she

31

was, swinging and swaying as she walked. She was fat,
like a little barrel, and she talked in a high whining
voice.

"Why didn't you come over and see me?" she complained to Myrto and me as soon as she drew near.

"Why didn't you come over and see me?" mocked
Odysseus, imitating Pipitsa's voice.

"All right for you," she whined. "If you make fun of
me, I won't let you in the barrel."

The barrel! We all leaped down from the tree. Ever
since last year Manoli had been begging her to ask her
father for one of the old wine barrels. Manoli had assured
us that the barrel would float, like a real boat. Which is
why we thought that it was really too bad that our great-
grandfather sold his warehouses. He could at least have
kept one barrel for us.

Manoli said angrily, "You're lying!"

"If I am, may I kiss my dead father and mother!" answered Pipitsa, making a cross with her fingers and kissing it.

That's why we couldn't stand her. She didn't just say
"Word of honor," like all the other children. It had to be,
"May I kiss my dead mother's face," or, "May they cut
me into tiny pieces and put me in a basket," and other ridiculous things like that.

We began to ask questions about the barrel. How big
was it? Where was it now? When could we get it? She just
stood there, looking at us, not saying a word, and it was
not until after she had chewed all the nails off one hand
that she finally said, "It's in our warehouse. My father
said that if we wanted it, we could take it right now."

But as soon as we started off, she halted us.

"Are you ever going to make fun of me again? Because if you are, we're not going."

"Nooooo!" we shouted in a chorus. "Noooo!"

"Swear!"

"We swear."

"No, no," she protested. "You have to say, 'May they hang us up by our tongues and cut out our guts and leave them sticking out.'"

"We're not going to say anything so stupid as that," Manoli replied, really angry this time. "Don't give us your old barrel."

"Oh, we don't want to have anything to do with her," Artemis said.

"And the whole summer, don't bother to come around us, not even once, begging us to play with you," Myrto added.

"We'll put a jellyfish on your back," Odysseus called out.

"All right," Pipitsa conceded. "Just say 'Word of honor,'" she wheedled.

So we said, "Word of honor." But she made every single one of us repeat it three times over.

Manoli had been right. The barrel floated like a real boat. We agreed that we had to think of a good name for it, so that when Niko came we could christen it.

Then a real argument started, because the barrel could just hold three, and Manoli and Myrto had ensconced themselves in it and had no intention of getting out again.

I only got in it once. Then I became bored waiting for my turn to come around again. I took a dive. My first swim that year! Swimming is the loveliest thing there is: taking long dives with your eyes open so that you can see the seaweed weaving on the bottom, like weird hands, and all the little fishes, and even the sea horses that swim upright, as though they were standing. And how light you get in the water! It feels like flying.

I don't know if there is any water in the world more beautiful than the sea at Lamagari. The pine trees, which grow right down by the edge, cast a shade over it. In some places the water is bright green, like a grape leaf; and in other places it turns bright blue. Certain spots on the bottom are covered with fine sand, and others with many-colored pebbles; and their colors are so bright in the water that you'd think they had been painted that very minute.

And to think that there are actually people who are born and exist and die without having once laid eyes on the sea, who have never seen Lamagari, not even a single time! Splash! I caught a big crab that was racing along to hide among the rocks. I ran out of the water to show it to the others, but they were all huddled together, staring at a huge dead fish stretched out on the sand. I threw my crab back into the water (it was a pity, because it had such a lovely coffee-colored spot on its back) and raced over to the fish.

"It's a dolphin," Artemis announced.

Manoli insisted that it wasn't, so we sent Myrto to get Grandfather.

"Of course it's a dolphin," he said as soon as he saw it.

Then he asked us, "Do you know the story of Arion and the dolphin?"

None of us knew it. So Grandfather led us over to the big rocks where the pine tree cast a thick shade and told us about Arion. Arion was a singer (in ancient times, naturally, because Grandfather only knew stories about the ancient Greeks), and he went on a voyage in a ship. The sailors wanted to steal everything he had and fling him into the sea. But he begged them to let him sing just one song before they threw him overboard. He took up his lyre and sang, and then leaped into the sea. But a dolphin that had been passing by was so enchanted by the song that it took Arion on its back and swam until it came to dry land, where it left him. And that land was our island.

"And so now you know," Grandfather said, "that the first inhabitant of our island was Arion."

But exactly on what beach the dolphin deposited him, Grandfather couldn't tell us. Just think if it had been Lamagari!

"I knew that dolphins love music," Artemis said. "One day a yacht sailed past out there and you could hear singing and guitars from it. And then I saw dolphins sporting behind it, a whole cloud of them!"

Manoli straddled the dolphin and began to sing. He had such a beautiful voice that, if the dolphin had been alive, it would surely have been enchanted. As I listened, I hoped that the situation would stop being so black so that Niko would take him to Athens to study music. This year Manoli was waiting for him so eagerly that he could hardly sit still.

When we got tired of playing with the dead dolphin, we went back to the barrel and then to the rocks, and after that to the beach. We didn't leave anything in Lamagari undone. You'd have thought we had to go away again at once, and wanted to squeeze in every single thing, right away.

We gathered crabs and shells and filled a whole basket with sea urchins. We broke their shells at the bottom, just the way Artemis had shown us, and sucked them out without getting pricked by their brittle spines.

That night we could barely keep our eyes open. When Great-aunt Despina said, "Go and wash your feet," we wished we were like the children from the shacks who could flop down, just as they were, on an old rag rug.

But by the time we had washed ourselves, we were wide awake again. And when we were in bed we started squabbling about what we would name the barrel. I longed to christen it *David Copperfield.*

"Stuff and nonsense!" Myrto burst out. "How childish can you get? Just listen to that! *David Copperfield* for a barrel!"

"Why not?" I insisted. "It's a lovely name. We'll write it on the barrel with red paint and everybody will see it from far away, and they'll say 'Look! There comes the *David Copperfield!* "

"Don't you dare mention it to the others," Myrto warned me. "Because they'll only laugh at you." And then we started to quarrel in earnest, so much so that

Grandfather came upstairs to find out what was going on.

"The Ancients said 'Contain thy wrath,'" he told us. "That means you must keep your anger inside you. When one of you is angry at the other, she must count up to ten before answering, and then her anger will have gone away."

Grandfather left the room, and Myrto started all over again.

"How could you ever have thought of anything so stupid?"

I started counting under my breath. "One, two, three . . ."

"Even little Aurora would split her sides," Myrto went on, since I hadn't replied.

". . . Four, five, six . . ."

"You see? You can't answer!"

". . . Seven, eight, nine . . ."

Myrto flung her pillow at me. The corner hit me right in the eye.

I didn't care any more about Grandfather's injunction to contain my wrath and counting to ten. I got up and gave her a pinch, she kicked me, and after that we sank back on our beds saying stubbornly, "Li-po, li-po!"

Peace descended. I was dying to know if she was still asleep. But in a little while I heard her whisper, "Ev-po! Let's call the barrel *Arion.*"

"Ev-po! *Arion,*" I repeated under my breath. "Ev-po." And I fell asleep.

⊒ 4 ⊒

Our Desperate Days. Stamatina.
Niko Arrives. Three Doleful Tales.

⊒ The days of the week sped by so quickly that we
didn't even realize it until they were over. Until Saturday
and Sunday: you would think each of them lasted for a
whole week. Perhaps it was because they were our Desperate Days. And as though everything else weren't
enough, we had to spend the whole of Sunday afternoon
with the Big Pest, Pipitsa, at her house. And we had to
remain very quiet on the veranda, near the grown-ups,
playing jacks. What else was there to do, with our moth-
ers and fathers close by playing cards or discussing boring grown-up subjects?

When we got up from our afternoon nap (yes, we even
had to take afternoon naps when Papa was at Lamagari!)
and saw those enormous organdy hair ribbons on the
chair—bows that made us look like candy boxes when we
wore them—and we remembered that it was still Sunday,
and that our Desperate Days weren't over yet, I was
really in despair.

We went over to Pipitsa's house and had to listen to her boring chatter about how many ruffles there were on the dress that was being made specially for her birthday.

Down below the veranda, Manoli and the other children were racing back and forth, on purpose, having the time of their lives. At one moment they decided to play hide and seek, and Manoli started counting out to see who would be "It." But instead of saying, "Five bubbles in the air, Mama, Papa, boom! Aberoom!" he said, looking around to see if we were watching, "Five hair ribbons in the air, Mama, Papa, boom! Aberoom!"

"I'll show him tomorrow!" muttered Myrto, pulling off her ribbon and stuffing it into her pocket.

Mama, it seemed, suspected what was going on, because she felt sorry for us and said she'd take us for a walk down by the sea.

"Don't go too far!" Papa called. "It's getting dark. You might slip on a rock!"

Fortunately, Pipitsa didn't come with us because her father, who also came only on weekends, said that he hadn't seen enough of her!

We went in the direction of the ancient sea wall. We didn't find any of the other children there, however. Who knew what they were up to? They might even have gone somewhere in Antoni's boat, while we were stuck like invalids on the veranda with the Big Pest. We were furious, and all our fury burst out over Mama.

"Why do you have to dress us up like dolls?"

"Every Sunday is just wasted!"

"We're not babies any more!"

Mama did not answer. She just sat and stared out across the sea. She was very young, just a wisp of a thing, and it was hard to think of her as a real mother. Anyone who saw us with our mother would think she was only our big sister. And even we had begun to believe it. It seemed that even the grown-ups didn't really think of her as our mother, because every time we asked her permission to do something, it wasn't enough for her to say "Yes." We had to ask one of the grown-ups, too—Grandfather, or Papa, or Great-aunt Despina.

"What sort of a mother is she?" Myrto demanded of me in a whisper. "She only wears a size five-and-a-half shoe!" Myrto already wore a size six.

Pipitsa's mother was something else again. She was very stout and had a double chin, whereas ours was slender and small. In a little while Myrto would be taller than she.

We longed for our own mother to be stout and matronly, to wear a corset with whalebones and laces that went through little metal holes. We had seen Pipitsa's mother's corset once, and it was just like that. And it was bright pink!

As we sat there, glowering, it suddenly occurred to me that she would have liked to be our sister, after all, to scramble over the rocks with us for crabs, instead of just sitting for hours on Pipitsa's porch. I suddenly felt sorry for the poor thing. Just think: every single day was a Desperate Day for her.

"Look!" Mama cried, pointing out to sea. "Look at the way that dog's swimming!"

It was Pipitsa's German shepherd.

"That's how the wildcat swam, only better," she went on.

We turned and stared at her in astonishment.

"I saw it once, before they killed it," she said. "I was about as big as Melia then. They were hunting it, and it just dove into the sea."

"And then what happened, Mama?"

"Then it vanished out of sight. They said it swam over to the opposite shore, to Turkey, back to where it had come from."

She had been our mother all those years, and only now had she thought to tell us that she had seen the wildcat when it was still alive!

"Great-aunt Despina says that it came over to our island to eat the sheep."

"Wasn't all of Turkey big enough for it?" Myrto demanded.

Then Mama pointed out to us the shore line, far off on the horizon. We could just barely make it out.

"Over there," she said, "on the Turkish coast, there used to be a Greek city with the curious name of Smyrna. When there was a war, the Turks burned it from one end to the other, and the city became like a desert. The fire spread as far as the forests and the mountains. Maybe it was then that the wildcat got frightened and ran away and leaped into the sea and swam over to our island. That was what the people did. They crowded into boats and ships and anything that could float and crossed over to our island to save themselves. The quay was jammed with people who didn't have any place to go, and they slept right in the streets."

"Do you remember all that, Mama?"

"Of course," she said. "And I remember as though it were yesterday the day Stamatina came and knocked on our front door."

"Stamatina!" we both cried at once.

"Just think, she's been our mother for years, and she never told us the story of Stamatina!" Myrto said, giving her sheet an angry kick.

We had been in bed for a long time, but we couldn't fall asleep. We had heard so many strange things that day that we were almost ready to admit that this particular Sunday had not been a desperate one.

"And when I think how nasty I was to Stamatina because she didn't know how many stamens an apple blossom has!" Myrto wailed. She was ready to burst into tears.

"And I told her to leave me alone the time she made me take along my jacket because it was windy!" I groaned.

But how were we to know, since we were considered to be too young, and nobody ever told us anything, that Stamatina's own family and her two children, girls our age, had been lost in the burning city? How were we to know that she alone had survived to make her way to our island, like the wildcat, wandering all day and night in the streets until finally one evening she knocked on the door of our house, when Grandfather opened the door and brought her inside? And from that day she had never left us.

When Stamatina came into our room to adjust the

shutters in case the wind rose during the night, we flung ourselves around her neck and started kissing her.

"Would you like me to give you the house that Great-aunt Despina's going to leave me when she dies?" Myrto asked.

"I'll give you Papa's briefcase, the leather one with the gazelle on it. Papa's going to leave it to me when he dies."

"Good God in heaven!" Stamatina gasped, crossing herself. "What's come over you two tonight with all this dying and giving?"

"Ev-po? Li-po?" The truth was that we couldn't say which we were. And we fell asleep without answering.

We were waiting for Niko. It was high time he came. June was nearly over. The ship from Athens had docked hours before at the pier in town. We had seen it steam into the harbor and could make out its name, *Frinton*, in white letters on its funnel.

At any moment now the *Crystal* would appear. Antoni had gone to town to pick up Niko and bring him to Lamagari. But in spite of all our begging, he would not take any of us with him, not even when we gave him our solemn word that we wouldn't fight about who would be first in the boat, but would cast lots.

"All right, don't take me!" Artemis called after him as soon as the *Crystal* had cast off. "And I won't cook for you any more, and I won't wash your shirts, and I won't mend them any more, either!"

"Never mind," laughed Antoni. "I'll get married in town, and I'll bring you home a stepmother!"

"Just try it! And I'll go over to the rocks and fall off and get drowned!" she shrilled after him.

Then the *Crystal* veered around and came back to the jetty. Artemis jumped in.

"Cheat!" muttered Manoli.

Antoni's brows beetled. He didn't say a word. And none of us dared ask to go along with them.

I don't know why, but all the children from the shacks have sorrowful stories, even sadder than *David Copperfield*. When I grow up I would like to be an author and write them. Myrto, however, has read somewhere that writers are born, not made.

As I watched the *Crystal* disappear into the distance, I thought to myself: what a pity! If I had been born a writer, I would write three doleful tales.

The First Doleful Tale
ARTEMIS

Often, just before sunset, Artemis says to Myrto and me, "Let's go to my mother's rock."

It is a high, steep crag. At its peak a small wild pomegranate has taken root. At its foot lies the sea. And from that rock last winter, Artemis' mother fell and was drowned. She was sick, and Antoni wanted to sell his boat so that he could send his wife to the hospital. But she did not want him to do that because, as she said, "the boat is our bread."

. . . And so she jumped from the rocks, so that her dearly beloved daughter might have bread . . . (That's

44

what I would write. Maybe I would cross out *"dearly beloved daughter"* and write just: *"her child,"* or *"Artemis."*)

When we reached the rock, Artemis would stand at its crest and start beating her chest and forehead.

"Oh, Mama! Why did you do it?"

And we would be so scared, Myrto and I, that we would hold on tightly to the pomegranate tree.

In Artemis' shack there isn't even a bed. When she and Antoni do not sleep in the boat, she just curls up on a rag rug on the floor. The only thing in the hut is a gold frame on one wall with a portrait of Great-aunt Despina, when she was young, in a ball gown. We kept that picture in our cellar because everyone said that it was so wretchedly painted. Niko, of course, teased Great-aunt Despina about it and called it "the scarecrow." One day, when Stamatina was cleaning out the cellar, she set it out in the courtyard. Artemis begged her for it a thousand times over.

"And now we have furniture of our own!" she said when she lugged it over to their hut.

Artemis' clothes are all things that Myrto has outgrown or outworn. Whenever Myrto wears something that Artemis likes very much, Artemis will say, "Don't sit in the sun, Myrto. All the flowers will fade!"

The *Crystal* was late in showing up. It would seem that Niko had gone to the house in town to see Papa and Mama. The children began skipping stones to pass the time. Manoli's stone skipped twelve times. I tried, but I couldn't do more than three. I couldn't beat Manoli, or Myrto, who never did under ten.

I went and sat on the edge of the sea wall and thought about

The Second Doleful Tale
(*with a Happy Ending*)
MANOLI

They say that when you dive in the deepest parts of the sea, where the sponges grow, you can be struck down by a strange illness they call "the bends." Then it may happen that you will never walk again as long as you live.

That is what happened to Manoli's father who went sponge diving in such deep faraway waters. Now he walks on crutches. All day long he sits in a chair outside the door of his shack, his hands idle, staring out at the sea.

I have never heard him speak. I am afraid of him. And once, in my sleep, I dreamed that instead of hands he had two huge sponges. Manoli's mother works in the warehouses that belong to Pipitsa's father. She washes out the wine barrels. When she finishes her work, Pipitsa's mother calls her to wash down the entire house, the courtyards, and the balconies. Niko, I don't know why, calls that "exploitation."

I believe that Niko will take Manoli to Athens with him. And so this doleful story will end with Manoli's becoming a renowned musician, his father's being cured,

46

and his mother's no longer having to wash barrels, but she will wear white gloves like the Mayor's wife.

The Third Doleful Tale
(*The Dolefulest of All*)
ODYSSEUS AND AURORA

I wonder what jail is like. I can picture a dark room—a tiny cell—and a slit of a window, all bars. You can't see any light, or even the sun, because the window is so high up that you can't reach it to see outside. Odysseus drew the window with its bars in the sand for us when he came back from the town where he had gone to visit his father, who is in prison. His father went fishing with dynamite, and they put him in jail because it is against the law. But if he doesn't fish with dynamite, he doesn't get enough fish and he can't earn enough to live on. Odysseus says that all the fishermen do it, only the ones who have enough money to pay the police to look the other way don't get caught.

Their mother left them and went to live in town. Sometimes, but very seldom, she comes back to visit, bringing a little doll, maybe, for Aurora. But Odysseus hides and doesn't want to see her.

"She left us, didn't she?" he says.

When we see him running along the beach to hide under an old upside-down boat, we know that his mother has returned to Lamagari.

"Odyyyyyysseus! Where are you, my darling?"

"Haven't you seen him anywhere?" she asks us. And we shake our heads.

47

Odysseus and Aurora live with their grandmother. She must be at least a hundred years old. She does her washing in the sea, and while she beats out the clothes with a big oar, she mumbles and mutters to herself.

"There she is!" Manoli shouted. "I can see her now!"

The *Crystal* had just begun to heave into sight. We waved our arms and screamed. "Nikoooooo! Nikooooo!" Soon we could hear him calling across the water.

"Hiiiiiiii!"

The boat approached and Artemis appeared wearing a straw hat with artificial cherries all around its ribbon. She had been waiting for Niko to bring it to her since the summer before. She had gone to town one day with Antoni and had seen a girl with a hat like that.

"I'll be so good, you'll see," she had told her father. "All I need is to wear a hat with cherries."

She was right, because now that she was wearing it, she sat very still and stiff and straight, like the Mayor's wife.

Niko hardly had time to jump out onto the wall before we were all over him, entangled in his legs, shouting at him and asking questions, all at once. He, in turn, examined us one by one to see how much taller we had grown since last summer.

Great-aunt Despina refused to permit us to come into the house with him. "Not with those feet!" she cried. "Stamatina has just finished washing the floor."

So we went off to our rocks to wait for him. Niko told us it wouldn't be long before he'd come out to find us. But just as we were moving off, we saw him look at

48

Manoli and frown. Niko had thick eyebrows that met over his nose when he was angry or thoughtful. They gathered until you thought they had filled his whole face. They were like the dark clouds that collect before a rainstorm. We would say then that Niko was clouded over.

"Manoli will stay and give me a hand," he said, "so that I can get unpacked quicker."

In the little cove beyond the house there was a big rock shaped like a shallow cave. That was where our rocks were. There was a large rock, just like a throne, and all around it stood smaller ones that you'd think the sea had worn down until they were like armchairs. Niko's place was in the throne, with us all around him. No matter how hot a day it was, it was always cool there.

We sat there paddling our feet in the water.

"What do you think Niko wants Manoli for?" Artemis asked.

Myrto said, "Maybe to tell him about taking him to Athens?"

I didn't say anything, but I knew that Niko wasn't telling Manoli about going to Athens, because Niko never clouds over when he has something good to say.

"Maybe the wildcat died!" Pipitsa exclaimed.

"You're the kiss of death," Myrto told her.

"I'll tell your aunt that you called me the kiss of death!"

"You can tell the Bishop, too, for all I care!"

"I'll tell her that you told me to tell the Bishop!"

Little Aurora, who very seldom opens her mouth to say anything, suddenly turned to Pipitsa and piped up, "And you're a tattletale!"

"I'll tell my father to take his barrel back," wailed Pipitsa.

I knew beforehand just how the dispute was going to end. Pipitsa and Myrto would come to blows, Myrto would win, and Pipitsa would run off to return in a little while with her mother. Her mother, however, never scolded Myrto and me, even if we were the ones who had been teasing Pipitsa. She always lit into the children from the shacks, even little Aurora. No matter how much Myrto and the rest of us would protest that it was Myrto's fault, Pipitsa's mother wouldn't pay us the least attention. Which was why Odysseus would have been perfectly justified in sticking his tongue out at her the instant she turned her back, since he would have been scolded anyway.

But fortunately, this time it didn't happen that way, because Niko and Manoli arrived at that moment. Niko sat down on the throne. I glanced at Manoli, and his eyes looked red, as though he had been crying.

"Well, what are you going to tell us about the wildcat?" Myrto demanded.

Niko burst into laughter. "Just look at those legs of yours!" he told Myrto. "Each of them has grown to be two yards long, and you're still asking to hear fairy stories! This summer I'm going to tell you only real stories. But now, first of all, let's have a swim."

It was always fun to go swimming with Niko. This time he started to teach us the crawl. He said we had grown too big to be still doing the dog paddle.

After that we stretched out on the sand. And then

Manoli asked, "What are the real stories you are going to tell us this summer, Niko?"

Niko did not reply at once. He only stared out across the sea as though he were thinking of something. He knitted his brows once more, clouding over. And at last he said, "I could tell you true stories about things that are happening in countries far away, stories about things you couldn't even dream of . . . stories that wise people and people like us should pay attention to. But I can't. Maybe next summer . . . Maybe even later this summer . . ."

"Tell us! Tell us! Why can't you?" we all cried together, impatiently.

"No," he insisted. "I'll tell you about other things."

We kept looking up at him, to see what he would decide to tell us. He picked up a handful of sand and let it sift through his fingers until at last all that remained in his palm was a piece of glass from a broken bottle, worn smooth as a pebble by the sea. Niko examined it, jiggled it up and down in his hand, and then, suddenly, he unclouded. He turned to us cheerfully and said, "Shall I teach you how glass is made? Or would you rather—" and he took from Manoli's head the cocked hat that Manoli had made for himself out of newspaper "—hear how they make paper?"

"You mean they *make* paper?" Odysseus said in astonishment.

"Everything is made out of something," Niko explained. "Well, then. I shall tell you how the wildcat makes paper."

One day when the wildcat was looking out of his blue eye and the black one was sound asleep, he set out to wander through the alleyways of the towns and gathered up all the old rags he could find. Then he went into the gardens and collected bark from the tops of the trees, and he stuffed everything into big sacks. He carried it all away and dumped it in front of a huge building with smoking chimneys. There was a big sign in front of the building with letters that said PAPER FACTORY.

Then a man came to the door. He picked up all the sacks, took them inside, emptied them into a vast caldron, and began to boil everything all together: rags, bark, and a pile of other rubbish that the wildcat had collected. Soon he had a thick pulp. The man spread it under some large rollers that he had, and rolled it out until it was just like a sheet of paper.

"Honestly? You mean that paper is made out of rags and rubbish?" exclaimed Odysseus.

"Yes," Niko answered.

"And my old underwear, with all the holes in it, can become a—a notebook?"

"Of course it can," Niko laughed.

"What a boring story," Pipitsa said, yawning.

But the rest of us liked it. Now, every time we read a book we know that there might be a piece of Odysseus' old underwear in it.

That evening, at supper, we learned that Niko couldn't take Manoli to Athens.

"Why can't you take him?" I asked. "Is it because the situation is very black indeed?"

Then Niko told a big lie.

"It's because I might have to go off on a trip."

We understood at once that it was a lie because, before he answered, Great-aunt Despina gave him one of her piercing looks, and he hesitated for a second before he spoke. After that, Great-aunt Despina told him, "You'll come to no good!"

"May your King flourish, along with the dictatorship that he'll bring in," Niko said.

Great-aunt Despina cut him off with a big, "Sssh!"

Grandfather started talking about the Golden Age once more, and about Pericles and democracy. And when Niko mentioned the dictatorship again, Great-aunt Despina hastily got up and shut the window.

She said, beside herself, "Somebody might be passing outside!"

"Why will Niko come to no good?" I asked Myrto as soon as we were in our beds.

But she had already fallen asleep.

⊒ 5 ⊒

Strange Things Happen. Our Cat Gets Its Name Changed. A Traitor in Our Midst.

⊒ Strange things were happening. Myrto and I were both aware of it. And it was these strange things that made this summer so different from the last. Other years, Niko never budged from Lamagari. Now, he was gone for hours. And when we asked where he had been, he would say, "In town, with my fiancée."

"What are you pulling those long faces for?" It was Stamatina who plunged into the conversation and pretended to scold us. "Do you expect him to play with you all the time? The man's engaged."

"Then what's your fiancée's name? Why don't you bring her to Lamagari for us to meet?" we wanted to know.

Then he started telling us stories. Like, for instance, how as soon as he arranged to bring her over to Lamagari, the wildcat opened its black eye and wouldn't let him budge a single step. And once, when we pestered him to tell us her name at least, his voice turned very low and mysterious. "What would you say," he whispered, "if I told you her name was Democracy?"

"Like our cat?" I giggled. Little did I know then how soon our cat would have her name changed.

When Papa came that weekend he was so jumpy and nervous that he found fault with everything. In the evening, when we were all having supper, I ran outside to find Blackie and Democracy, because Stamatina said that it had begun to drizzle. I found Blackie right away, but Democracy was nowhere to be seen. Then I started to call, "Demooooooocracy!" so that she would hear me and come home. I didn't even have time to come inside before Papa grabbed my wrist and hauled me in. I thought he was angry because I had gotten up from the table. But it was really the cat.

"Either you get rid of it," he said, "or you change its name. I have absolutely no intention of losing my job at the bank."

So we shortened the cat's name to Demmy. But what we had heard was really very queer. How could Papa lose his job at the bank because of a cat?

Myrto and I asked Niko if he was going to change his fiancée's name, too.

"No," he answered, laughing, "a thousand times, no!"

But when Niko wasn't off in town, he played with us just as he always had. When he was there at Lamagari we didn't ever get bored. He could always invent some new game. Then there was the wildcat and all the stories about it. And that summer, Niko told us lots of stories: boring stories, as Pipitsa called them, but you could learn a lot of things from them. We learned how glass is made, as well as paper. And furthermore, Niko explained why something as heavy as a barrel can float in the water, while a shoe, which is so light, sinks as soon as you throw it into the sea.

Best of all were the wildcat stories he told us at night. As soon as it grew really dark, and the stars shone brightly, Niko and we would stretch out on a high flat-topped rock. It seemed to us then as though the sky came closer and the stars could almost touch us. When the sky was very black, Niko said that it was the shadow of the wildcat crossing from the Big Dipper to the Little Dipper, and from Mars to Venus. That was how all of us, even little Aurora, learned how to distinguish all the stars and call them by their names.

And then, one day, something happened and the stories about the wildcat changed, and were never the same again.

Maybe it was Odysseus' fault, although he didn't mean it. After all, he had never gone to school and didn't know any geography.

We were all sitting in the sand with Niko. The sun had just begun to set. Niko said that the sunset wasn't as beautiful anywhere else in the world as it was at Lamagari. Then he started to sing a song in a low voice, in a language that none of us knew.

"What song is that?" Manoli asked at once. He picked up the tune right away.

"It's Spanish," Niko answered.

"What's Panish?" Odysseus asked.

"Spanish, stupid," Myrto corrected.

Niko scowled because Myrto had called Odysseus stupid.

"It would be better, Miss Know-It-All," he said, "if instead of making fun of people because they don't know something, you taught them instead."

Then he found a stick and drew a map of Europe in the wet sand. In the lower left-hand corner was Spain.

Myrto and I knew about Spain because we had read about Don Quixote, the Knight of the Mournful Countenance, who was a Spaniard. It would be lovely, I thought, if Niko would tell all the others now about Don Quixote and his groom, Sancho Panza. And maybe he would tell us how instead of riding his horse, Rosinante, Don Quixote rode the wildcat.

"What do the words of the song mean?" Manoli asked.

Niko did not answer at once. Then he said, "I would tell you the story of Don Quixote of La Mancha—" and he made a dot on the map, to show us La Mancha "—but now Don Quixote can no longer wander through the cities and the countryside of Spain, because there is a war there.

"That's Madrid, the capital of Spain," he said, making another dot on the map.

"There is a war," he went on. "On one side there are soldiers from all over the world: Englishmen, Russians, Frenchmen, Americans. And they sing the song I was just singing. On the other side there are bullies with black shirts."

"Did you go to Spain?" wondered Artemis.

He laughed. "No. But the wildcat goes, and then he comes and tells me."

I thought: was this one of the stories about things that were happening in countries that were far away, one of the stories that we had to pay attention to?

"What side is the wildcat on?" Manoli wanted to know.

"When his blue eye is awake he is with the ones who sing. But when his black eye is open, then he is with the Blackshirts."

With our bare feet we jumped all over the part of the map where Niko had shown us that the Blackshirts were. We jumped and jumped until it was all stamped out.

Then Niko looked steadily at each one of us and said, "That's our secret."

We gave him our word of honor that we wouldn't breathe it anywhere. Pipitsa went into her usual, "May I kiss my dead— may I see my whole family in their coffins first!"

At night, in bed, we started singing Niko's song very softly. We only hummed it because we could only remember two or three of the strange Spanish words. It seems, though, that we weren't singing as softly as we thought because Niko heard us and burst into our room.

"Are you out of your minds?" he said, pretending to scold us. "Didn't we say that it was our secret? Do you want the grown-ups to hear?"

"And if they do hear, so what?"

"They'll want to know where you learned it, and it's a song of Democracy."

"You mean," I said, "they could fire Papa from the bank?"

"Maybe," he laughed. Then he grew serious. "It's my fault. I forgot that you're only kids."

After he went away we couldn't fall asleep.

Everything was so strange! Why could they dismiss Papa from the bank, just because we were singing a Spanish song? Demmy came and curled up at my feet. And because of our cat's name!

"Ev-po?" Myrto whispered. "Li-po?"

"Ev-po! Ev-po!" The grown-ups could do all the strange things they liked. "Ev-po! Ev-po!" It was lovely spending the summer at Lamagari with the other children and with Niko. "Ev-po, ev-po!" Because we were at Lamagari, the most beautiful place in the whole world.

But the next day everything was "li-po."

It all began on Sunday morning, even though we were sure it was going to be a wonderful day because Papa and Mama hadn't come to Lamagari and we had escaped our Desperate Days. Niko left in the morning for the town, but it wasn't to see his fiancée. Now we knew where he went. He had gone with Odysseus to see Odysseus' father in jail. Saturday night Stamatina had been baking cookies and cheese pies for them to take to him. Great-aunt Despina was terribly cross because Stamatina hadn't had time to wash down the verandas. We went to Artemis' shack.

"Come on, give me a hand with my laundry," she said to Myrto and me. "Not that you know anything about it, but just to keep me company, so I don't get bored."

I had taken along *David Copperfield* to read to Artemis while she did her washing, and Myrto had brought a basket of fresh figs. They were a very special kind of figs, and Artemis was wild about them. There wasn't even a single fig tree near her shack, only rocks and sand. These figs didn't grow in any other part of Greece, or maybe anywhere else in the whole world, only in Lamagari. They were bigger and thicker than ordinary figs. When you picked them in the early morning they were icy cold from the dew, and they stayed cool all day long. They were sweet and sticky, and when you peeled them they gave off a strong lovely fragrance.

"If they asked me to be Queen of England," Artemis would say, "I wouldn't go, because they don't have them there."

We couldn't help her much with the laundry. We just watched her, astonished at the speed with which she scrubbed every garment until it was as white as paper. I didn't even have time to open *David Copperfield.* Artemis did not know how to read, but she recognized the book from its cover.

"Do me a favor," she said. "Don't read me such sad stuff because I'll start crying and then I'll never get my washing done."

Then we all took the laundry over to the rocks where we spread it out to dry.

"Listen!" Artemis said suddenly, jerking her ear out toward the sea.

In a little while the noise was clearer, and a motorboat appeared, cutting through the water. When it came closer we could see that in it were the Bishop, the Mayor, and Mr. Amstradam Pikipikiram.

"That's why we escaped Pipitsa today," Myrto said. "They're having visitors."

But instead of veering toward the sea wall, the motor-boat came straight toward the rocks where we were standing.

"Run and tell your aunt we're coming to see her," the Mayor shouted to us.

The motorboat turned toward the sea wall. Myrto and I started running to tell Great-aunt Despina the news.

"Come back quickly!" Artemis called after us.

We found Great-aunt Despina in the kitchen. She was in her house robe and she and Stamatina were preparing stuffed tomatoes. As soon as we told her about the visitors she got very excited and started pacing the kitchen with a tomato in her hand. Then she told us to bring her best dress and her good shoes.

Grandfather, who was out on the veranda where he had spread his Ancients out on a little table, got up at once and went upstairs.

"Very strange," he said. "What can they want at this hour of the morning?"

"They're not coming here for our good, you can be sure of that," muttered Stamatina.

"Don't talk foolishly!" Great-aunt Despina cut in. "They're coming to inspect their warehouses."

We could hear their footsteps on the courtyard tiles. Great-aunt Despina went to the door to welcome them.

Myrto and I were perishing of curiosity. What were the Bishop and the Mayor doing here on Sunday? They came very seldom to Lamagari, and when they did they always went to Pipitsa's house. And there was Pikipiki-ram, who didn't have any warehouses at Lamagari.

We knew that eavesdropping was wrong, but then visitors like that didn't arrive every day. We stayed in the kitchen to help Stamatina stuff the tomatoes, because we knew that the visitors would sit in the rear courtyard, which was cool; and from there we could hear everything through the kitchen window.

In the beginning they talked about how hot it was in town, and how cool it was in Lamagari. They praised Great-aunt Despina's arbor that covered the whole courtyard like an awning. And finally, after each of us had stuffed three tomatoes, the Bishop spoke. He was talking about the wildcat! He said that they knew everything. They knew what was hidden behind the wildcat!

After that, the Mayor and Mr. Amstradam Pikipikiram went on to talk about Niko's stories, even about how paper and glass are made. ("Just listen to that!" said the Mayor. "Do those peasant children have to know how you make glass and paper?") And then they talked about the Big Dipper and the Little Dipper; and finally, their voices turning ominous, about Spain: about how the wildcat goes back and forth bringing news . . . But they were going to find out who that wildcat was, and——

"You must tell him to stop all that, Mrs. Despina. Otherwise, we will soon be obliged to take matters into our own hands."

"Tell who? The wildcat?" I whispered in astonishment.

"Ah, it's Niko they mean, silly," Stamatina said, nudging me.

"Niko!"

What happened after the visitors left is not to be described. Great-aunt Despina nearly fainted, and Stamatina rubbed her forehead with cologne. Grandfather came downstairs; Stamatina told him how the billy goat (the Bishop) was after the stuffed wildcat in the glass case. Grandfather didn't know what she was talking about. Great-aunt Despina heaved a sigh.

"Ah, the trouble he's causing us! He'll come to no good end. Ah, his poor mother!"

The grown-ups had begun acting strangely again. But Myrto and I could only think of one thing: where had the Bishop and the Mayor and Pikipikiram found out about Niko's stories, especially the one about Spain which we had all solemnly sworn to keep secret?

We rushed out of the house and raced to Grandfather's vineyard where Myrto began chirping like a cricket. That was our signal. It wasn't long before Manoli and Artemis and little Aurora were there. We told them the news. Manoli looked at each of us in turn and said, "One of us is a traitor."

We all stared without saying anything. Only Artemis spoke.

"I'll pull all the hairs out of her head, one by one!"

Because, of course, we all knew that no one but Pipitsa could be the traitor. Then we said that we would bury her in burning sand. Or we would put her in the barrel, nail it over, and let it float out to the open sea. But then Manoli said that first we had to make sure that it was Pipitsa. Myrto ran off to call her, saying that we were going crabbing. After she left, Artemis, Aurora, and I all burst into tears, without really knowing why.

"What are you babies crying about?" Manoli said, but his voice was shaky.

We walked along in silence as we went off to catch

crabs. Only Pipitsa talked. She said she was going to ask her Papa for another barrel so that we wouldn't have to squabble about who would have first turn, and then we could name the new barrel *David Copperfield,* just as I wanted. We let her chatter on. When we reached the cove, Manoli and Myrto grabbed her arms and Manoli fixed her with his eyes.

"Why did you tell?"

"I? What did I say?" Pipitsa said excitedly. She had begun to breathe heavily.

They must have given her arm an extra hard squeeze, because she screamed, "I'll tell my father what you did. He'll put you all in prison!"

"What did you tell them about Niko's stories?" Myrto asked angrily.

"I said— I only said— I didn't say anything!" she wailed.

We could all see that she was a liar. It made no difference, her going to school and her father's owning all those warehouses. The children from the shacks didn't know how to read or write, and sometimes they used bad language, but none of them ever told lies.

Then we all got angry, even little Aurora. We pushed her down and started covering her with sand. She shrieked, but she couldn't budge because Manoli and Myrto had tight hold of her arms and legs. Artemis, Aurora, and I threw handfuls of sand over her as fast as we could, to bury her. The sand was baking hot, and the sun blazed over our heads, but all we could think of was that Niko was in trouble with the grown-ups, and it was all the fault of that Big Pest, Pipitsa.

A shadow came and stood over our heads.

"What are you doing there?"

It was Niko. He pulled Manoli and Myrto away and began excavating Pipitsa, who by now was buried under a small mountain. The only part of her that hadn't been covered was her head.

We had never seen Niko so angry. He did not utter a word. He picked up Pipitsa, who was half-sobbing, washed her off with sea water, and then grimly regarded each of us in turn.

"Aren't you ashamed of yourselves!" he said at last.

"You don't know what happened, Niko!" Manoli was the first to speak. "That's why you're mad at us."

"I know," he answered.

Pipitsa started swearing all over again. "May I kiss my dead mother's cheeks if I ever do it again!" And she started telling, without anyone's asking her, how they had bought a bath for her doll, with a real water cistern; and they had promised her a toy piano that really played; and all she had to do was tell them what Niko had said when he was playing with us. And if we didn't bury her she wouldn't tell them a single thing more, even if they promised her a bicycle.

Niko, however, was not angry with Pipitsa, who was a traitor and a liar. We were the ones he turned on.

"What do you mean, trying to bury someone alive? Only the Fascists do that."

"Who?"

"The black-shirt bullies who don't believe in democracy and freedom, and want to force everyone else to do as they think!"

65

We were in tears all the way home, even Manoli.

We couldn't touch our dinner, even though there were shrimps, which Myrto and I both love, as well as the stuffed tomatoes. But neither did the grown-ups seem to have much appetite. None of them said a word. Finally, Great-aunt Despina spoke.

"When are you leaving?" she asked Niko.

"Day after tomorrow, with the *Frinton*," he replied.

Niko, leaving! Myrto kicked my ankle under the table. It was our signal. We gobbled our fruit as fast as we could and got up from the table.

"Don't bother to go into the kitchen," Great-aunt Despina said. "Stamatina doesn't know any more than that, so you'll get no information out of her."

We turned to stone. Grandfather and Niko burst into laughter.

"What a nose your Aunt Despina has!" Grandfather said. "She knew right away where you were off to."

But we were cheered by Niko's laughter, because it had made us terribly unhappy that up to now he hadn't spoken to us, not a solitary word.

"The wildcat," Niko said, "has its black eye really open now. That's why I'm leaving."

"Please, Niko," Great-aunt Despina said nervously. "I don't want to hear that creature mentioned again, ever!"

Then Niko really began to laugh. "Are you too beginning to believe, Auntie, that your wildcat comes back to life at night?"

"You're incorrigible!" she scolded. But her expression was already somewhat softer.

⧉ 6 ⧉

The Sails of Theseus, the Dictatorship, and the Secret of the Half-armed Windmill.

⧉ Niko did not mention Pipitsa to us again. He didn't say a single word. It was as though nothing had happened. He played with us until late at night. And he decided that, since the next day would be his last at Lamagari, he would take us on an expedition to the *castro,* the old fortress. We would leave at seven in the morning. Antoni would lend us his boat. The ship was due to dock in the town at dawn, Antoni would go to pick up his passengers, and then he would return to Lamagari. This expedition helped to console us and the other children for Niko's leaving. Grandfather was going to come along with us. Otherwise, Great-aunt Despina wouldn't let us go anywhere.

"So I'm going under guard?" Niko said, joking. Then he added, "It's a lot better, of course, to go under Grandfather's guard than under that of the police!"

We didn't mind Grandfather's going with us. We knew

that he would have one of his Ancients with him. He
would sit somewhere in the shade and read all day long.
At the most, he'd tell us some myth.

At dawn the next day we were up and ready. But even
when the sun was high overhead, Antoni and the *Crystal*
had not shown up.

"Maybe the ship hasn't come yet?" I said.

"I heard its whistle even before daybreak," said Artemis.

At last the boat appeared. Antoni, however, did not
seem to be in any hurry. He pulled slowly on the oars,
since there wasn't any wind at all for him to open sail.

"Something's happened, you'll see," said Artemis, looking worried. "When my father makes a promise, he always keeps it."

"What could have happened, Artemis?" Niko laughed.
"He probably ran into some friend in the coffeehouse and
forgot."

Grandfather chuckled. "And he didn't put up his sails,
for us to see if it was a white one or a black one, and
know if he was bringing good news or bad."

"Why black sails?" we asked.

"Let me tell you the myth," Grandfather said, "so you'll
know."

We were delighted, because that way the time would
pass more quickly. Impatient as we were to see the *Crystal* tie up, Grandfather with his myth was able to make
us forget it for the time being.

"Well," he began, "in Crete, in very ancient times,
there lived a king named Minos. Minos built a great

cellar with endless passages and rooms. Whoever entered it could never find his way out. It was called the Labyrinth. And in it, Minos kept a bull which was called, naturally enough, the Minotaur. King Minos conquered the Athenians in war, and the tribute he exacted from them was that every nine years they had to send seven maidens and seven youths to Crete, to be devoured by the Minotaur."

At that moment Manoli shouted, "There it is! It's coming!"

"The Minotaur?" cried little Aurora, frightened.

"I was wrong," Manoli said after a moment. He had thought that the craft which showed up on the horizon was the *Crystal.*

"And just like Manoli," Grandfather went on, "the King of Athens, Aegeus, stood straight up on a rock to see from far off when the ship with his son, Theseus, would appear. For this time Theseus had gone along with the other youths and maidens to try to slay the monster. Many youths before him had tried to do this and had never returned. The ship that bore him away had hoisted black sails, as a symbol of his going to meet his death. Aegeus had instructed the captain to raise the ship's white sails if his son returned alive. In that way he would recognize them from far off, and understand.

"Theseus went to Crete and slew the Minotaur. But on the return voyage the captain was so happy that he forgot to change the ship's black sails."

"Can it happen that somebody forgets out of happiness?" I asked.

"Of course it can happen," Niko answered. "Just as somebody can die for joy."

"For joy?" Artemis exclaimed in astonishment. "You'd never catch me forgetting, or dying, just for joy!"

"When Aegeus saw the ship approach," Grandfather said, ending his myth, "and made out the black sails away out in the sea, he was certain that Theseus had been killed by the Minotaur. And he fell from the rock into the sea and was drowned. Which is why we now call it the Aegean Sea."

If the *Crystal* had had black sails, they should have been hoisted. That's what Grandfather said later, when we went home. We didn't go on our expedition: not because the sun was too high by then, but because even before Antoni was out of the boat he said, "Niko, we have a dictatorship now."

In August, at Lamagari, the air at noon was full of the sound of cicadas. Every time Papa came to Lamagari he would get annoyed because they interfered with his nap. But we couldn't imagine Lamagari without the cicadas. We lay on an old blanket under a pine tree and listened to them. I caught one and closed my fingers around it. It chirped madly.

"We have a dictatorship now," I whispered to it, and let it fly away to tell all the other cicadas.

"I wonder what will happen now?" Myrto said.

"Niko said that now everything will be different," I told her.

At home, everything had already changed, from the moment Antoni brought the news. First of all, they let us do anything we wanted. We ate without washing our hands first. Nobody reminded us to take our afternoon naps. And no one said a word when they saw us drag out the old blanket and go outside. Even Grandfather was changed. For the first time in our lives we heard him speak crossly. And to whom? To Great-aunt Despina!

"If the King wants a dictatorship, that means it was necessary," Great-aunt Despina said.

"You talk like a fool, and it would be better if you didn't discuss such things!" Grandfather growled.

Great-aunt Despina burst into tears. And, I don't know why, she turned on Niko.

"Now that there's a dictatorship, do you think they'll let us children do anything we want?" Myrto asked.

"Let's try," I told her. "Let's go and find the others, even if it is noon, and the 'hour of repose,' as Aunt Despina calls it."

We hadn't had time to set off before Niko came up to us. His face was very sad, and his eyebrows were so closely knitted together that they made a thick black bar across his brow.

"Girls," he said, "you're too young to understand this. But Greece will always remember and regret this day. Do you know today's date?"

"It's the fourth of August, 1936," Myrto answered promptly.

Afterward, Niko left for the town, but we couldn't tease him any more and ask him if he was going to bid farewell to his fiancée.

In the afternoon, Mama and Papa arrived. Papa gave

us a hundred commandments, and of course we couldn't possibly remember them all. "You must be careful what you say." "You must never utter the word 'Democracy.'" "You must not discuss grown-up affairs," and a whole heap of other must-nots. Because otherwise he might lose his position in the bank, and then we would have to live in a shack, summer and winter.

"Wouldn't it be marvelous if he did lose his job!" I said to Myrto. "Then we'd be able to stay in Lamagari with the other children!"

But Myrto looked lofty and said, "I think we ought to do whatever they say so that Papa doesn't lose his job." And before I could answer, she snapped furiously, "You can stay here and be a peasant, but I want to go to school."

Papa had brought the newspapers with him. They were full of big photographs of a fat man with glasses, and Papa said that this was our Dictator.

"He looks just like a frog," muttered Stamatina.

Papa gave her such a look that she didn't say anything more.

I don't know why Mama kept kissing us all the time, and her eyes were filled with tears. Really, the dictatorship was a terribly strange business.

Niko came home late at night, after we had gone to sleep. When we woke the next morning, they told us that he had left. We were furious at Stamatina because she hadn't awakened us. He had gone, it would seem, at dawn, so that even Artemis hadn't seen Antoni get up to take Niko to the ship with his boat.

"What do you think of that! He didn't even say good-by."

"You're a wicked old thing," we told Stamatina. "You didn't wake us up in time."

Even Great-aunt Despina lit into her. "You let him steal away early in the morning, like a thief, without saying good-by to anybody!"

Stamatina explained that Niko had told her not to upset us.

"He shouldn't have left now," Grandfather said. "They could telegraph a message to Athens, and the minute he walks off the ship——"

Grandfather did not finish the sentence because Great-aunt Despina gave him her piercing glance. We wanted to know what would happen the minute Niko walked off the ship. "Tell us, Grandfather," we clamored. "Tell us, please!"

"Run off and play and don't bother about matters that don't concern you," Great-aunt Despina said, and we knew that the subject was closed.

I don't know why it is, but every time the grown-ups don't want us to find out something, they send us off to play.

We went and found Artemis. She sat on an old log outside their shack with her back turned to Antoni, who was standing beside her.

"What are you mad at me for?" he was asking her imploringly. "Since that was what Niko wanted?"

As soon as Artemis caught sight of us, she leaped up and ran toward us.

73

"I'll buy you a red calico dress when I go to town again," her father said in a coaxing voice.

"I don't want it," she retorted sulkily. "And I'll never speak to you again as long as I live."

Then she turned to us. "Let's go, girls."

"Artemis, I'm going to fry fish. Come back in time, so that we can eat early," Antoni called after us when we had started off.

"I'm never going to eat again as long as I live!" she shouted back.

Myrto and I looked at each other. How we longed to be able to say sometimes to Great-aunt Despina, or to Papa, "I'll never speak to you again as long as I live!"

The three of us made our way along the shore. But we didn't feel like doing anything, not even like burying the Big Pest alive, even if they'd let us. We were mad at Niko, though, because he hadn't let us do it the day before. And then we were furious at him for having stolen away at dawn, like a thief, as Great-aunt Despina said, without saying good-by to us.

Soon we saw Manoli racing toward us. He was panting so hard that at first he could hardly speak.

"I was looking everywhere for you," he got out at last. "Stamatina sent me to call you."

"Can't she leave us alone?" stormed Myrto. "Isn't it enough that she didn't wake us this morning?"

Manoli turned to me. "Listen, Melia. You have to come. She said for Artemis and me to come, too."

Myrto flung out, "Then why didn't she tell us this morning?"

"Oh, let's go," Artemis said. "It's not as though we have anything to lose."

We found Stamatina in the kitchen. The instant she saw us, she signaled to us to be very quiet.

"Your aunt has a headache and has locked herself in her room. She said, 'I don't even want to hear a fly buzz.'"

"Is that why you wanted us?" Myrto said, pouting.

Stamatina did not answer her. She merely stuck her hand in her apron pocket and drew out a bit of paper folded in fours. She handed it to Myrto and told her to read it.

Myrto read it aloud.

"This afternoon you will go searching among the rocks, behind the throne. Open the mussel shells that you will find there. The Wildcat."

My heart was pounding wildly.

"I found it in a pot," Stamatina said when she saw us staring at her open-mouthed. "I took off the lid to start my cooking, and I saw it lying there on the bottom."

We knew that the story of the wildcat was only a fairy tale. But sometimes, when Niko was telling it, we had asked ourselves: "Could it be really true?" And now we had a letter from the wildcat himself, in Stamatina's pot!

"Well, what are you going to do?" she asked us. I couldn't imagine why, but she had a sly look on her face. "Are you going?"

"Of course we're going!" Manoli said. He turned to us. "Aren't we?"

Poor Manoli. Perhaps he was the one who minded

Niko's going most of all. It wasn't just because Niko hadn't taken him with him to Athens, but because when Niko came to the island he often went in the evenings to sit with Manoli's father. And Manoli's father, who never spoke to anyone, would talk to Niko for hours, and his gaze would no longer be fixed emptily on the sea. Sometimes Niko would take his guitar along with him, and Manoli and his father would sing together.

When that happened I wasn't afraid of Manoli's father any more. He would smile, and he would appear so changed that I expected him to throw away his crutches and run around.

"We'll meet at four o'clock," Manoli said, looking at a large man's watch on his wrist.

It was Niko's watch! He must have given it to Manoli before he left.

"Well, are you going?" Stamatina asked again; and, without waiting for an answer, started telling us what to do. "The four of you will go. Don't take the little ones, Odysseus and Aurora, with you. As for Pipitsa, don't spill a single word! Be sure none of the grown-ups sees you. Don't say anything to anyone about the letter. You heard what the Mayor said: 'We'll find out all about the wildcat, and then——'"

"No one will find out anything," Manoli said.

"Swear!"

"Word of honor!" the four of us said as one.

I could hardly bear the thought of going to the rocks and seeing the wildcat, large as life, waiting there for us and looking out of its sky-blue eye. But supposing its black eye was the one that was open?

76

It was a long time to wait until afternoon. Artemis pulled Myrto and me aside to tell us a secret.

"Listen, you two! Can't you invite me to eat dinner with you? I told my father that I wasn't going to eat again as long as I live, but my insides are already rumbling."

"I'll ask Stamatina," Myrto whispered, "since Aunt Despina is sick."

I said in her ear, "Ask her about Manoli, too."

Stamatina didn't require much begging. "There's half a roast of lamb, with potatoes, left over. No one had any appetite yesterday. Your grandfather's left for town. Your aunt's sick. You can eat right here in the kitchen so as not to disturb her with your chattering."

We leaped on her and started hugging her.

"Oh, Stamatina, you're so good, so terribly good!"

"Good, am I?" she muttered. "Do you think it's *my* food I'm dishing out?"

If only, we thought, we could eat every day with Manoli and Artemis! Artemis was so funny. She sat down to eat wearing her hat with the cherries, and acted just like a grown-up lady. And she ate I don't know how much! She held out her plate haughtily for Stamatina to fill it up again.

"Won't you please pass me a little more meat, because in our house we love the poor little lambs so much that we eat them only once in a blue moon."

Stamatina grinned. "Ah, Artemis! You ought to be an actress!"

"Ah, Artemis! You ought to be an actress!" Artemis mimicked; and she was exactly like Stamatina. Then she pretended to be Great-aunt Despina and scolded us. And after that she was Pipitsa's mother, and then Pipitsa herself with all her airs and graces. Stamatina laughed so hard the tears rolled down her cheeks.

Then we all helped Stamatina wash the dishes. All except Artemis, that is. She sat stiffly in a chair.

"I wash and sweep in my own house every day," she said. "Today I am an honored guest."

If we hadn't been so sad over Niko's departure, it would have been the best meal of the whole summer. What a strange thing sadness is! When you're terribly sad about something, you feel sure that the sadness will never go away your whole life long. It was just like that that morning when I woke up and saw that Niko had gone, and I felt that I would be terribly unhappy at least until the summer was over. And then, later, when we found the note, and Artemis started being funny, the sadness began to go away, bit by bit; and all that was left was the excitement of what we would find at the rocks.

At the rocks, behind the throne, we found a basket. It was covered. We opened it and saw that it was filled with grapes and bread and other things to eat.

"What do you suppose that means?" we said, wonderingly.

Manoli said, "Let's find the shells, as the letter says."

We searched carefully, and in a little hollowed-out place by the throne, we came upon three big mussel shells. Two of them were still alive, because they clenched when we tried to open them. The third held a bit of folded-up paper on which was written: "Take the basket and go to the half-armed windmill. If anyone sees

78

you, say that you're going on a picnic. But, better still, don't let anyone see you."

We had never really lived in a story before! Things under a dictatorship couldn't be as bad as Niko said. There had been a dictatorship since yesterday morning, and to us children it had only meant that marvelous and exciting things happened.

We knew where the half-armed windmill was. The windmills had always been there, at Lamagari. Grandfather could remember when they had been busy, flailing the air with their sail-like arms. But for years now the ships had brought flour to the island, and so the windmills were unused and deserted.

"Just supposing," Artemis said, "the windmill has changed into some kind of magic palace and is waiting for me to be a queen!"

Manoli broke into her flight of fancy. "Give me a hand with the basket now," he said. "And if you turn into a queen we'll all drop on our hands and knees and bow before you."

We trudged along without talking, taking turns lugging the basket. And it seemed that we all had the same thought: what were we going to find at the half-armed windmill?

We didn't believe in ghosts, even though Pipitsa had sworn ("May you cut me up in tiny pieces in a basket!") that one day when she was going for a walk with her father, she had seen, from a distance, down by the windmills, a ghost. It was wearing an enormous white hat and in its hand it held a branch with silver flowers. Maybe the other children were reminded of it, because when we climbed the hill and reached the crest, as soon as we could make out the windmills down below us, we stood stock-still. It was as though our feet had been nailed to the ground.

Manoli was the first to start the descent, holding on to the basket. The hill wasn't very high, but the back part of it suddenly got all rocky, and in order to go down to the windmills our legs got terribly scratched. The wildcat couldn't have chosen a worse place to send us. There were two windmills, and they stood in a small valley with thick shrubbery and a narrow strip full of rushes. The mosquitoes gathered in thick clouds. They attacked our arms and legs. All around the windmills there were old shoes and pieces of rusting iron. The stone walls of the windmills were cracked. One of them had no arms left at all. The other had only half an arm, and it looked more like a pointing finger.

We drew near the half-armed windmill, but we couldn't make up our minds to push the door open.

"It's not locked," Myrto said. She gave it a little shove with her foot.

The door gave a loud creak. It sounded like the jackals that we could hear at night, sometimes, howling in the distance.

"I'm scared," Artemis had the courage to admit.

If I hadn't been too ashamed, I would have said so too.

"Look," Manoli said. "Stairs."

We peeked through the opening and saw a twisting staircase.

"Let's climb it," Manoli suggested cautiously.

"I'm not going anywhere," said Artemis.

Manoli opened the door all the way. It creaked fearfully. And then, suddenly, a low song could be heard.

Niko!

And we could hear footsteps coming down the stairs. He halted on one of the steps and smiled down at us.

"What's the matter? Have you all turned to marble? Welcome to my castle!"

We all gaped. So all this had only been a game? And everyone had agreed to take part in it, just to make the game seem more real, even the Bishop and Pikipikiram, just to make it all more believable?

If we hadn't seen in the newspapers the picture of (I had forgotten the Dictator's name) the frog, as Stamatina called him, we would have thought that the dictatorship was a kind of grown-up joke, that it hadn't really happened, since, instead of terrible and awful things happening, everything had become even more exciting and amusing for us children.

"All right, Niko. Admit that it's all a game!"

Niko knitted his brows, and again they were like a thick straight dark bar across his face.

We realized that it was not a game.

"Let's go upstairs," Niko said.

The stairs opened onto a tiny room which just barely had space for a mattress. We all squatted on the mattress, and then Niko told us everything. He hadn't left with the *Frinton* because in the town he had learned

from friends that the Mayor had telegraphed to Athens
to have him arrested as soon as he stepped off the ship.
So that was what Grandfather had wanted to say when
Great-aunt Despina cut him short!

Now he was in hiding, so that they would think he had
left. Otherwise, he would have been arrested in Lamagari.

I stood there, and I felt a shiver of perplexity and
fright creep over me. Was this what dictatorship meant, I
wondered: that Niko could be arrested and put in prison
just because the Mayor sent a telegram to Athens about the
stories Niko told us?

As from a long way away I heard Niko go on to say
that he would have to remain hidden in the windmill for
several days. After that, he would go to the town and
hide there until he could arrange to leave the island
secretly.

"Everything," Niko said, "depends on you. As you see,
it's not a game any more."

We would bring him food in the basket which Stamatina would leave at the rocks during the night. So that sly
Stamatina was also in on the secret! And if the police
ever came to Lamagari, we were not to go down to the
windmill, but just climb the hill above it and chirp like
cicadas.

Myrto and Artemis were terribly enthusiastic. Even my
own shiver of fear blew away. And Niko had said that it
wasn't a game! This was a real game. We had secrets
from the grown-ups. Only we would know that Niko was
hiding. And we were going to see him secretly, and not
tell anybody, not even if they skinned us alive, as Artemis

82

said. And, finally, we were going to help Niko, and everything depended on us!

Dusk had begun to fall. We could barely make each other out in the darkness.

"Aren't you afraid, all by yourself?" Artemis asked.

"Have you forgotten about the wildcat?" Niko answered. "As soon as it's night, he comes and keeps me company."

Manoli said suddenly, "Let me stay with you tonight."

"No, Manoli, even though I would like some company. The wildcat, you see, doesn't talk."

At least with the coming of the dictatorship we could do as we liked. Otherwise Great-aunt Despina would have given it to us for getting home so late. On the way home we had to pass in front of Pipitsa's house.

"Where were you?" she called from her veranda. "I was looking for you all afternoon."

We hadn't noticed her, so now that she put the question so suddenly, we didn't know what to say. Fortunately, she didn't ask us again but started bragging.

"My daddy is going to be the German Consul on our island because he went to school in Germany. He says what the Germans are doing under their leader, Hitler, should be an example to us all. Mummy says our house is going to be the German Consulate, and we'll give lots of parties. And I'm going to have a pale blue organdy dress!"

"You can tell us everything tomorrow," Myrto said. "We have to go home now."

"But you didn't say where you were!" Pipitsa called after us.

But we were already too far to answer.

When we reached the house, we could hear the "Pa, vou, ga, de, ke, zo, ni." Grandfather had come back from the town. We were in a hurry to run to Stamatina, but he detained us on the veranda, just in order to tell us the myth of King Midas, who had donkey's ears. When his barber came to cut his hair and saw the donkey's ears, Midas told him, "You have to keep it a secret from everybody." But the barber, who was very talkative, was ready to burst because he couldn't tell anyone. So he made a little hollow in the ground and called down into it, "King Midas has ass's ears!" A reed took root in that hole. When the wind blew, the reed swayed and whispered, "King Midas has ass's ears!" And so everybody knew.

"Grandfather knows," Myrto said when we were in our beds. "You can be sure of it."

"About Niko?" I wondered.

"Yes. That's why he told us the myth about King Midas."

How odd Grandfather is! Even without knowing about King Midas we would never have told our secret to anyone.

Stamatina came into our room to shut the windows.

"It smells like rain," she said.

"Why would they arrest him as soon as he got off the ship?" I asked her in a whisper.

"Be quiet!" she answered, and came and sat on my bed.

As soon as Myrto saw her do that, she came and burrowed in beside me.

"Really, why?" she asked.

84

"Because there's a dictatorship, and Niko's against it. That's why. And it would be better for you if you didn't go around asking so many whys."

"Then why don't they arrest Grandfather?" Myrto asked. "He doesn't like the dictatorship either."

"Niko's different."

"Why different?" we asked, both together.

"Niko's a freedom fighter."

"What's that?"

"I said what I've said, and that's enough for one night," she answered, bridling.

All the same, I still wondered what it was.

When Stamatina went away, Myrto said, "Let's sleep together," and made herself more comfortable in my bed.

I moved over to give her more room.

"Ev-po? Li-po?" she was the first to ask.

"Li-po, li-po," I answered.

"Why li-po, Melia?"

"Because everything is so mixed up."

"Well," said Myrto, "then I say 'li-po,' too."

If the story of Pinocchio is true, then Artemis' nose should have grown three yards long. She told so many lies! It seems, however, that there have to be good lies and bad lies, and the good lies don't make your nose stretch.

It was three days since Niko had hidden in the half-armed windmill. And our Desperate Days had set in; and what Desperate Days! Aside from the fact that we couldn't go to see Niko, our father was very irritable.

He said, "That story about the wildcat going back and forth to Spain could have consequences." That was what Amstradam Pikipikiram had told him. He had told Papa to tell Great-aunt Despina that it mightn't be a bad idea to open the wildcat's belly to see if anything was concealed in the straw stuffing.

What an idea, to cut open the wildcat's belly!

"I'm afraid," Papa said, "that they'll send a message to Athens, and Niko will have a real mess of trouble on his hands."

If only Papa knew, I thought.

After that, Pipitsa came to visit with her mother and father. It had been very difficult for us to speak to the Big Pest ever since she betrayed Niko, even though he said that it wasn't her fault.

At one moment, when we were thoroughly fed up with hearing her prattle about her daddy and the Consulate and that German dictator named Hitler, we caught a glimpse of Artemis racing past under the veranda. Myrto hung way out over the railing to call her, but she was already too far away. In a little while, there she was again. And then she was off once more. This happened several times.

"What's gotten into her?" Myrto whispered to me.

"You'll see," I said. "She probably wants to tell us something."

We were dying of curiosity. But how were we to get away from the Big Pest? She clung to us like an oyster, as Myrto says.

When Pipitsa finally left, along with her mummy and daddy, it was already too late. Artemis had long since vanished. We went out to the courtyard, to the pump, to wash our feet. And there she was again.

"I got stiff waiting for you," she said. "And if I don't tell you, I'll explode!"

Before we could even ask her what it was all about, she began telling us. She had gone to the town with Antoni. They had summoned him to the police station, to ask him if he had actually taken Niko to the ship.

"'Yes,' my father said. 'I took him,'" Artemis went on. "But he said it just like that, so bluntly, that I was afraid they wouldn't believe him. I don't know what came over me, but without anybody's asking me, I said how I was in the boat too; and when the ship started moving Niko was out on deck and he waved to us. 'Ehhhhhhhh, Niko! You forgot your glasses!' I shouted. And he called back, 'It doesn't matter. You can have them as a present!'"

"What glasses did he forget?" I wondered.

"In the boat, silly. My father took him in the boat so that anybody who saw them would think they were headed for the ship. And he forgot his dark glasses. I wore them today when I went to town. Oooh, they make everything look so different! You can stare at people as much as you like without their catching on. Do you think Niko'll let me keep them?"

"What else did they ask you?" we demanded impatiently.

"'What did Niko tell you about the wildcat?' A policeman with one stripe on his sleeve threw the question at me, very sudden. I played dumb. 'What's a wildcat?' 'An animal, like a tiger, that Mrs. Despina keeps in a glass case.' So I answer, 'It's the first time I ever heard of anybody putting an animal in a glass case.' The one-striper bursts out laughing. Then he pulls himself together and puts on a very serious face and asks me, 'What did he tell you about Spain?' So I tell him, 'I never heard of the lady.' The one-striper bursts out laughing again. Then he gets serious again and starts asking me some more. "Do you love our King and our new ruler?' So I say, 'Oh, I only wish I was a queen!' And then another policeman puts in, 'She's got something missing upstairs.' He said it low, but I had my ear sticking out. 'Are you telling me the truth?' the one-striper asks me finally. So I answer, 'Of course I am, Colonel!' I tell him."

"Myrtoooo! Meeeeeelia! Are you still washing your feet?"

It was Papa calling us.

"We're coming," we called back, and rushed back inside with our feet unwashed.

Anyway, they weren't very dirty because we had been sitting on the veranda all afternoon.

We had just gotten into bed when Mama came upstairs to our room to say good night to us.

"Mama—" I began. And then I stopped short. If only she had been a fat, motherly-looking mama. If only she hadn't been so young, with feet even smaller than Myrto's! Then Myrto and I would have been able to ask her so many questions. And she would have told us what Stamatina meant when she said that Niko was different, that he was a freedom fighter. She would have told us, too, if it was right for Artemis to tell so many lies, and if it made any difference that the lies Artemis had told had been to policemen. And she would have told us if it

88

counted as a lie when we gave answers that didn't make any sense, every time we were asked about Niko.

"What do you want to tell me?" Mama asked, bending over to put her arms around me.

"Which is better: to be a child or a grown-up?"

"I don't know. I was happy when I was a child."

"Did you have secrets from the grown-ups?"

"Of course I had."

I thought about it, and finally I decided that it was really too bad that Mama wasn't a child any more. Then she would have been in on our secret and she would know all about the half-armed windmill.

It wasn't easy for all four of us to go to see Niko together. Pipitsa would see us, and so would the two little ones, Odysseus and Aurora. So we decided to go two at a time: Artemis with Myrto, and Manoli with me. This time it was our turn to go. We were glad, because we had a letter that Antoni had brought from the town. Every time we went there Niko asked us, "Did you bring a letter?"

We climbed the little hill. We had reached the top and were about to start the descent into the little valley when we suddenly heard shouting. We turned. And then, a little further on, we caught sight of two policemen shoving a man along in front of them. When his footsteps dragged they started hitting him all over his head and shoulders. Terrified, we flopped down among the bushes and watched. It looked to us as though they were heading for the half-armed windmill. The man began to scream. The whole valley seemed to quiver with the sound of his voice, but the policemen only beat him harder. Suddenly a stream of bright blood spurted from his head and ran down over his face. I had never seen so much blood in my whole life. I shut my eyes so as not to see any more. Manoli waited long enough to make sure that they were not going toward the windmill, and it was only when the shouts and screams were very far away that he nudged me and we crept out of our hiding place. While we were running downhill I cut my foot on a jagged rock. I wanted to cry, but I was ashamed to in front of Manoli, who would only say that girls are all cry-babies.

But when Niko saw me he was alarmed. I hadn't realized that my foot was covered with the blood that kept pouring out of it. And it wouldn't stop. I remembered the man we had seen being beaten by the policemen; and without wanting to, I began to shake all over. Niko cleaned out the cut with alcohol from a little bottle he had. Then he bound up my foot with my clean handkerchief and picked me up in his arms like a baby. Niko had heard the shouting and had been frightened, thinking that something had happened to us on the way.

"You're only children," he said, "just children. I forgot that."

"We're not children at all," Manoli told him. "And if the girls are scared, I'll come by myself."

"No, Manoli," Niko went on. "You're still children, and you ought to be playing children's games. But the way things are now, we grown-ups need you."

I didn't say anything because I saw that the handkerchief which Niko had tied around my foot had turned bright red, and I was terrified of blood.

Niko turned to me. "You will get Stamatina to take you to town at once. They'll have to give you an anti-tetanus shot. There's all that filth around here."

It was true. There was the smell of mold and rot everywhere. Suddenly everything seemed hideous to me: the cramped room with the mattress on the floor where Niko was living; the half-arm that nearly covered all of the windmill's tiny window; the mosquitoes that flew all over, biting. I burst into tears.

"Take me home, Niko," I begged. "I can't go back alone with Manoli."

He looked worried. "Does it hurt a lot?"

"Yes," I said. But I didn't know if it hurt, or if I was afraid of the anti-tetanus shot, or, even more, of the man with the broken head and the blood flowing and the policemen that were beating him up.

"Take me home, Niko, please!" I sobbed.

"Let's go," Niko said then, getting up.

I stopped crying at once. He took hold of me to help me down the stairs.

"Suppose somebody sees you?" Manoli said. "The policemen could be somewhere near."

"But you said they went to the other side of the valley. We'll go through the forest, even if it's the long way around. It's beginning to get dark. Nobody will see us."

I wanted to be able to tell Niko to stay there, but I was too frightened. We started off. Niko carried me because I couldn't put my weight on my foot.

"You should eat more," he joked. "I feel as though I'm not carrying anything. It's a good thing it's not Myrto, instead of you. She'd break my back!"

Manoli went on dumbly beside us. It had grown very dark now, in the woods. If Niko hadn't been there I would have died of fear. It made me shiver just listening to the dried-out pine needles snapping, crack-crack, under our feet, and seeing the branches slowly sway back and forth like giant hands, ready to grab at you. How different everything is at night! We had played in that forest thousands of times. We knew every bush and tree in it. But now it was like some strange wild place. Beside Niko, however, my terror shrank until it was no bigger than a walnut.

Niko made jokes, talked about the wildcat, spouted nonsense, just as though he were a boy. For a moment I imagined that everything was the way it had been before. We would go home now, with him. We would eat our evening tomato soup and fried cheese with big air bubbles in it, and he and Grandfather would tease Great-aunt Despina about her royal families . . .

As soon as we were out of the forest, and our castle hove into sight, Niko put me down and told Manoli to give me a hand. Then I was reminded that everything had changed. I would have to tell Great-aunt Despina a thousand lies; and, later, just as many more to Mama and Papa about where we had been and how I had hurt myself.

"Tell Stamatina to take you to town tonight," Niko said before leaving us. "It's dangerous."

He took two steps. Then he came back and kissed me.

"Don't be afraid, Melissa, and everything will be over."

"When you grow up," Niko used to tell me, "I will call you Melissa. Melia doesn't mean anything." Maybe I had already grown up?

Manoli helped me walk, but he didn't say a word.

"How are we going to explain being so late?" I asked him. "How are we going to explain my hurting myself?"

There was no word from him.

"Why don't you say something, Manoli?"

"Because you're a scarecat. Because on the way back Niko could run into those policemen and they'd beat him up, just like that man. They could even kill him."

"Meeeeelia!" "Meeeeeelia!"

They were the voices of Stamatina, Grandfather, Great-aunt Despina.

Manoli called out, "Here we are!"

Artemis and Myrto ran up to meet us first so that they could tell us that everyone had been worried. And they had told the others that they hadn't seen us because Artemis had wanted Myrto to read to her out of a book that Manoli and I both knew already; and we were bored and went away. I kept on crying and couldn't talk. But Manoli told them everything: how I was a scarecat, and that Niko was in danger, all on account of me. He didn't have time to say any more because then Grandfather and Great-aunt Despina and Stamatina all arrived.

Manoli just cannot tell lies, not even for Niko. I was howling. And so it was Artemis who had to lie once again. She said that we had gone to the far cove for limpets and I slipped on a rock and cut my foot, and we were late because it was so far and I couldn't walk. The grownups all started talking at once. Great-aunt Despina said, "We've let them go around too much on their own. All we need is for their father to hear about this!" Grandfather said, "They're children, and it's only natural for them to fall and get hurt." Stamatina said, "By the time she's married, she'll have forgotten all about it."

Grandfather picked me up in his arms and carried me home.

"Tell them to take you to town," Manoli whispered in my ear.

But I had already made up my mind. I wasn't going to say anything, even if I had to die. Then Manoli would never be able to call me a scarecat again.

Great-aunt Despina washed out my foot and put iodine on it. I clenched my teeth and didn't scream.

"It's a good thing that Melia cut herself on the rocks," Grandfather said. "Otherwise we would have to take her for an anti-tetanus shot."

"Why do they give anti-tetanus shots?" I asked.

"Because when somebody cuts himself where there's a lot of dirt, it's dangerous."

"Can you die if you don't get a shot?"

"Don't be afraid, Melia," Grandfather laughed. "You cut yourself in the sea. The sea contains iodine, and iodine is the best antiseptic."

So I was going to die. I was sure of it now. I had cut myself where there was so much filth around. And maybe, when he heard about it, Niko would say, "Melia was a brave girl. She was not afraid to die." That would show Manoli . . . But if anything happened to Niko on the way back, what good would it do if I died? And it was all because I was a scarecat. The children wouldn't come near me any more, and I'd be just like Pipitsa. No, it would be better to die.

They put me to bed. And when I said "Li-po" to Myrto, I thought how now she wouldn't have anyone to say "Li-po, ev-po" to any more; and I felt sad for her.

I was feverish all night long. I saw a ravine with a man walking in it. The policemen were hitting him. Blood was streaming. It was Niko! "It's Melissa's fault, Melissa's!" he shouted. Then the wildcat with its black eye came and pounced on me . . . I screamed.

"Melia, Melia, what's the matter?"

I opened my eyes and saw Myrto beside me. I was burning with fever.

"Don't—don't call anybody," I said. "I'll sleep now."

I slept. And by morning, I still hadn't died. The fever had ebbed. My foot hardly pained me at all. I just couldn't put my weight on it. Grandfather stretched the hammock out under the pine trees. Myrto dragged out three thick books.

"I won't go swimming either," she said. "I'll stay with you."

We hadn't even had time to open the books when we saw Manoli racing toward our castle. What was he up to? I wondered. Soon he appeared again, with Stamatina this time, and they came over to where we were. She placed her hand on my forehead and asked me anxiously, "How are you feeling, my little chick?"

Then she turned on me angrily. "Why didn't you tell

me to take you to town? Don't you know you might have died? Ah, that lousy dictatorship, that gets little children mixed up in messes like this!"

Myrto turned ashen. "You mean Melia could have died?" she asked.

Then Manoli said it was all his fault because he had called me a scarecat. He opened his fist and showed us a brilliantly colored clamshell that he had hidden in it. It was pinkish, with gold and green stripes. I had never seen such a lovely one before, ever.

"It's a present for you," Manoli said. And he gave it to me.

What a good thing it was I hadn't died! Everybody made a fuss over me and gave me presents. It's lovely, now and then, to nearly die, just so long as you don't really. I suddenly sat up.

"What about Niko?" I asked Manoli.

"He's all right." He smiled. "And he says to tell you to get well."

That meant that Manoli had gone back the night before to the half-armed windmill, to make sure that nothing had happened to Niko. And he hadn't been afraid, all alone, at night!

I didn't go to see Niko again. At first it was because my foot hurt, and then because after a while he left Lamagari. He went "someplace" in the town. That was what Stamatina said.

Every day there were policemen all over Lamagari. One day they even came to our castle and pried into everything, even into the box where we keep salt. Stamatina knew one of them. He was very fat and his name was Pandeli. When the other two who came with him went outside, Pandeli stayed on for a while in the kitchen. Stamatina gave him coffee.

"Aren't you ashamed of yourself," she said, "poking around in other people's houses?"

"Do you suppose I enjoy doing it?" he replied. "It's our duty. And tomorrow we have to trail the kids to see what they play at and where they go."

The plan had been for Niko to leave for the town in a few days. We were to act as lookouts while Antoni picked him up at a remote cove. He would have to make his getaway in the daytime because at night the harbor-master's motorboat might be patrolling to see if they were fishing with dynamite.

But when he heard what Pandeli had told Stamatina, Antoni said that there was no time for delay. Niko would have to leave for town the very next day. And Artemis figured out how we could fool the policemen. We would pretend that we were being very careful they didn't see us, and we would go toward the *castro*, the old ruined fortress which was directly opposite the point that Antoni's boat would have to pass with Niko.

We didn't go to the *castro* to play very often because it was so far from the sea. And then, too, we were a little afraid. Everyone said it was haunted. We set out at noon, with the sun directly overhead. When we had made sure that Pandeli and the other policeman were on our trail, we started marching toward the *castro*.

You have to climb sixty-eight stone steps in order to reach it.

"Ehhhhh, you children! Where are you off to?" Pandeli shouted, halfway up. He sat down, puffing, on one of the steps.

He called out again, "And where are you taking that baaaasket?"

We had brought the basket along with us, the one we had used for Niko's provisions. We were lugging it up the steps in such a fashion that all Lamagari could catch sight of it.

"We're taking presents to the ghost of the *caaaaastro!*" Manoli called back.

Pandeli and the other policeman stared and started puffing up the steps once more. All that remained of the old fortress were its high stone walls and a staircase that opened on to a sort of terrace with turrets and embrasures. In the middle of this staircase there was a landing; and on the wall side, an opening with a rusty iron railing. Where it led to, no one knew. Two feet inside the opening you could feel a gust of cold air, and it was so dark that you couldn't see your own nose.

"Our ghost is in here," we told Pandeli, showing him the pitch-black gaping hole.

First Myrto shoved her face into the hole.

"You have to chant the exorcism," Artemis told her.

And Myrto began to recite, "Pa, vou, ga, de, ke, zo, ni . . ."

"My God, what's she saying, that one?" the other policeman cried out to Pandeli. "Stop her! She's warning whoever's in there to beat it!"

"Are you trying to be funny, Mr. Policeman?" Artemis

98

said. "That's an exorcism, just to get it in a good mood. The ghost never goes away from his castle!"

"We'll have to search," he told Pandeli.

Pandeli didn't show much enthusiasm for squeezing into the hole. But the other policeman had already vanished inside it. Pandeli tried to strike a match.

"It's no good trying to make a light," Manoli told him. "The air from the hole will just blow it out. The ghost hates light."

"Pandeliiiii! Are you coming?" The policeman's voice could be heard calling from the depths.

"Present!" Pandeli shouted. He crossed himself and squeezed inside.

We sped up the stairs and emerged onto the terrace.

Far down below us the sea lay spread out. A single boat with a snow-white sail was cruising about in it. Antoni also had a red sail for the *Crystal*, but we had agreed that if everything went well he would hoist the white one. And Antoni didn't make a mistake, like the captain of Theseus' ship.

Soon, from below, we could hear loud sneezes.

It was Pandeli and the other policeman who had emerged from the hole. We could hear their boots thundering, vroom, vroom, on the paving bricks of the courtyard. We leaned out of an embrasure and watched them secretly. Pandeli had pulled out a huge red-checked handkerchief and was blowing his nose.

"We didn't catch any ghosts," we heard him say. "But I caught a cold!"

We had never played a better game any summer! But

that was our last game on Lamagari. Until it was time to leave for the town to go to school, the days dragged drearily along: without Niko, without the wildcat, without even a single secret. And up until the moment we embarked in the *Crystal* to go back to the town, nothing interesting happened, except when Artemis' hat with the little cherries fell into the sea and the waves carried it out to where it was too deep for us to rescue it. We just watched helplessly as it floated like a big jellyfish in the distance, fading like the whole past summer out of our sight.

We would see Manoli and Artemis all through the winter. Artemis was going to come to the town now and then so that Great-aunt Despina could teach her sewing. That's what she said. I don't know if she really liked to sew. I think she was jealous when she heard that Manoli was coming. Grandfather was going to coach Manoli every other day so that he could take the annual examinations as a "Home-instructed Pupil." It wouldn't be easy, of course, for Manoli to go back and forth in the cold and rainy weather. But Manoli was not afraid of anything. When he grew up he was going to be, like Niko, a freedom fighter.

But only Manoli and I knew that. Since the time I cut my foot, Manoli and I had become close friends. He told me all his secrets. He too was summoned one day to the police station and they asked him about Niko. It was there that they told him that a freedom fighter was someone who was trying to overthrow the dictatorship.

"Well, since Niko is fighting for freedom, that's what

I'll do too when I grow up," he told me. And he made me swear not to tell anyone, not even Myrto. To be perfectly truthful, it made me very unhappy not to be able to tell Myrto. It was the first time in my life that I had a secret from her. It's marvelous to have secrets from the grown-ups, secrets that only the children know. But I don't like it one bit to be the only one who knows something, when you've given your word not to tell it, not even to your own sister.

When we got into our beds, before we fell asleep and before saying "Li-po? Ev-po?" I was always afraid that, without meaning to, I would let the secret escape and reveal it to Myrto. That was why, to relieve myself a little of the burden of it, I did just what Midas' barber did. I scooped out a little hollow in the sand, and I said into it three times, "Manoli is going to fight for freedom." Then I covered the little hollow over with damp sand and I stamped it down with my foot.

But all that night I couldn't fall asleep. I was afraid. I said to myself, "What if some reed takes root in it and all the reeds whisper my secret?" The next morning I didn't even stop to wash, but rushed right out to the beach. Once I saw that the sand was bare, as always, I was calm again. Great-aunt Despina saw me coming back and she scolded me.

"Aren't you ashamed of yourself, at your age, already traipsing around at all hours of the day?"

Later, Myrto asked me, "Where did you go, really?"

"I told a secret in a hole in the sand and I wanted to see if any reeds were growing there."

"You're too old to do such baby things!"

"Why is it so babyish?" I answered angrily. "Isn't that what Midas' barber did?"

"Oh, that's only a fairy tale."

"No, it isn't!"

Several days went by. And then, one night, Myrto asked me, "What was the secret you buried in the hole?"

I pretended to be asleep, but I was "li-po, li-po," because I had secrets from her.

We were already looking forward to the coming winter. We would go to school, we'd have new girl friends, we would see Manoli and Artemis when they came for their lessons. It wasn't going to be dreary at all. And maybe something strange with Niko and the wildcat would start happening again.

In spite of all that, I felt my heart tighten when the *Crystal* was bearing us away and Lamagari started to disappear from our gaze. I stood straight up near the bow and I said good-by to it. I said, under my breath, "Farewell, farewell, dear Lamagari, fairest spot on earth, the best place in the whole world!"

Myrto came and stood beside me. And before the last point of land on Lamagari vanished, we cupped our hands and shouted with all our might: "So long, Lamagari!"

Only the echo came back to us. "Lamagariiiii!"

Part Two

⊒ 1 ⊒

Owls and Kings. Wrecks and Tortures.

⊒ We always loved the first days when we went back to the town. They were all waiting for us again: our room and our games and the wildcat. He stood in his glass case and it seemed as though, the moment he saw us, his sky-blue eye came to life.

This year, however, there were two things that we were not permitted to mention in the house: Niko and the wildcat.

"He's put us to enough trouble," said Great-aunt Despina.

And you couldn't figure out whether she meant Niko or the wildcat.

The day after we had returned to the town, and Stamatina had been given the key of the case by Great-aunt Despina so that she could clean its glass sides, Stamatina called us into the parlor.

In the beginning I was afraid to stretch out my hand to pat the wildcat. Myrto touched first his whiskers and then his claws. "They're like real ones!" she breathed.

I touched them too, then. The claws were hard and turned outward. Then I patted him. His fur, when you stroked it one way, was smooth and glossy. Myrto said his eyes were glass. I didn't touch them, but I bent very close and it seemed to me that they were staring at me. They had a weird glitter, one of them as blue as the sky, and the other one jet-black. The wildcat's mouth was half open, showing his long pointed teeth.

"Look!" exclaimed Myrto. "There's something in his teeth!"

She cautiously inserted her hand and drew out a small slip of white paper.

WELCOME TO TOWN. ENJOY SCHOOL.
The Wildcat.

We turned and stared at Stamatina who was vigorously attacking an armchair with her dust rag. No matter how much we crossed our hearts and begged her to tell us what she knew about Niko, and if we were going to see him again, she only pressed her lips stubbornly together.

"Don't you get me mixed up in this," she said. "Didn't your aunt say, 'The wildcat and Niko are forbidden subjects'?"

We did not ask her again for many days, not because we believed that she really didn't know anything, but because we were in such a state about school, which was to open in a week. Mr. Karanasis' school was not far from our house. It stood right on the quay. The classes in the upper story could see the ships coming and going. On the balcony there was a sign with huge black letters:

PYTHAGORAS PRIVATE SCHOOL
John Karanasis, Director

Mama and Grandfather took us for enrollment. I don't know why, but when we entered the director's office, I felt my heart tighten. Stuffed birds stood on shelves all around the room, and on the walls hung pictures of all the kings of Greece. In the middle of the wall, right over a little shelf with a stuffed owl, hung an enormous photograph of our dictator. I stared at it. Really, Stamatina was right: he looked just like a frog.

Mr. Karanasis, the director, sat at his desk and he looked solemnly at us, without smiling. He had on a black suit, like the one Grandfather wore when he had to go to a funeral. First of all he spoke to Mama about the discount he was giving us on the tuition.

"As you see, I am not concerned with making a profit. What interests me is having children of good family in my school."

Myrto and I exchanged a glance. It was the first time we had heard anything about our being of good family. Mr. Karanasis then began asking us questions about arithmetic and grammar; and, seeing that our answers were correct, he turned and said to our grandfather, "I congratulate you, sir. You have given them an excellent preparation."

We thought the examination was over, but suddenly Mr. Karanasis pointed to the kings on the wall and asked Myrto to name each of them. Myrto knew them all. On winter nights, when it was very cold, Great-aunt Despina would let us sit in her room, where a big brass brazier burned, and she told us about the kings and queens. She had a big album full of photographs of the Royal Family, and she would show them to us one by one. Myrto loved the album, and knew all the pictures by heart, so it was a lucky thing Mr. Karanasis picked on her. But I found Great-aunt Despina's album very boring, because when they are real kings and queens, and they aren't in fairy stories, they're not very amusing. I would wait from moment to moment to hear the "Pa, vou, ga, de, ke, zo, ni" which meant that Grandfather had finished his reading and might be in the mood to tell myths.

It wasn't easy for me to decide to leave Great-aunt Despina's room because it was so warm, and after she had finished with her Royal Families she would open a cupboard and give us quince paste and tiny green oranges preserved in syrup. In Grandfather's room, not only was there no fire, but he kept the window wide open. And he didn't have any cupboard with sweets.

But he knew about Admetus and Alcestis and about Perseus and Andromeda, and myths—myths without end! So I would slip out, leaving Myrto behind, absorbed in the album. As soon as Grandfather saw me come into his room he would shut the window and give me a blanket to wrap myself up in. In the beginning I would shiver with the cold and think of Great-aunt Despina's brazier with its flaming coals and Myrto spooning out the sweets. But when Grandfather started talking I had no more regrets, neither for the warmth nor for the sweets I had given up.

Of course, Mr. Karanasis didn't know all this. And he

didn't know that Grandfather loved Pericles and democracy, and couldn't stomach any kings, not even an ancient one, much less, of course, the present-day one, who wasn't even Greek by birth but had been, as Grandfather said, foisted on us from Denmark.

So the director repeated, "I congratulate you, sir," thinking that Grandfather had taught Myrto about the kings. Then he turned to Myrto. "And if you continue to be such a good student, we'll soon make a leader out of you. Our ruler has established a Youth Organization!"

Grandfather and Mama did not utter a word on the way home. Myrto and I chattered away. Myrto's feet hardly touched the ground, she was so elated because they were going to make her a leader, even though she still had no idea what it was she was going to be a leader of.

"Did you understand what they were going to make me a leader of?" she asked Grandfather.

"We will discuss it at home," he answered, and continued in silence along the street.

But at home we didn't discuss anything; or, rather, there was a lot of discussion that we couldn't make head or tail of. Because from the time the dictatorship had come, Papa said one thing on account of his position at the bank, which he didn't want to lose; Grandfather said something else, on account of his Ancients and his loyalty to Pericles and democracy; and Great-aunt Despina said something else again, because she loved anything to do with royalty. Only Mama didn't say anything, but we realized that secretly she agreed with Grandfather. All the same, it seemed very funny to me that the grown-ups were having such a serious discussion about whether Myrto could be a leader. Great-aunt Despina kept insisting that Myrto would make a lovely leader. Nor did we understand what the Youth Organization was that Grandfather said was such a terrible thing to compel children to join.

At night, when we went to bed, Myrto was brimming with happiness. She teased me for being younger and not having decided, as yet, what I would be when I grew up.

"And what are you going to be? You don't know either!" I answered furiously.

"Of course I know. I have decided to become a leader."

"That's not a profession!"

"It most certainly is!"

I wanted to tell her that I was going to become a writer, but she would only have repeated that you can't become a writer, you have to be born one.

"And you, were you born a leader?" I demanded, storming.

Myrto perched on the brass bedrail and replied haughtily, "A leader isn't like a writer. Anybody can be born a leader."

Stamatina found her there on the bedrail when she came into our room to close the shutters.

"It's going to come down in buckets. God have mercy on anybody who's voyaging tonight!" she murmured.

I suddenly thought of Niko. Where could he be? I wondered. And there hadn't been any message from the wildcat.

"Could Niko be voyaging tonight?" I asked.

"What made you say that, my child?" she exclaimed, startled.

"Because you said, 'God have mercy on anybody who's voyaging.'"

"He's not voyaging," Stamatina said solemnly, then. "But he's riding the storm."

After that she closed her mouth tightly, and we could ask as much as we liked about Niko and what had happened to him. It did no good. Stamatina's lips stayed sealed.

"Li-po, on account of Niko. Ev-po, on account of going to school," Myrto said when we were alone again.

"Li-po, li-po," I answered, because I wasn't glad about the school any more. Maybe it was all because of the kings and the stuffed owl.

On the first of October the street was filled with children in blue and black smocks. We wore blue ones with white collars. My teacher was named Miss Irene and the boy who sat next to me, sharing the same desk, was called Alexis. I wanted to talk to him before Miss Irene came into the classroom, but each time he sat in such a way that his back was almost turned on me. I noticed that his smock was threadbare and old and that his shoes were worn down all the way at the toecaps. I thought that we would never become friends. I told myself, if only Manoli, instead of Alexis, were going to the same school as I!

The lesson was already under way when the door opened and Mr. Karanasis came into the room.

"Miss Irene," he said to the teacher, "you are going to have one more pupil, a daughter of one of the best families in our community."

It was Pipitsa! And Mr. Karanasis went on to say a thousand and two nice things about her. How could he know that she was a traitor and a liar?

At morning recess, Pipitsa was very gracious to me. She had been going to another school, she said; but when she learned that we were going to this school, she had raised such a fuss that they had let her come here. And now I was going to have the Big Pest near me all winter long.

At the end of recess Alexis came up to me. He was very tall and thin and pale.

"What's your name?" he asked.

"Melissa."

"I heard that fat girl" (he meant Pipitsa) "call you something else."

"She called me Melia. That's my nickname."

"What do you want me to call you?"

"Whatever you like."

"Melissa, then. Melia doesn't mean anything."

"That's what Niko says!"

"Who's he?"

"He—he's a boy in our neighborhood," I stammered. And I blushed on account of the lie.

Then Alexis asked me something I hadn't expected. He asked whether we paid regular tuition, or had a discount. I was ready to be annoyed. What did it matter to him what we paid at school? But he didn't give me time to answer. He only said, almost in a whisper, "I'm here with a discount. And if my arithmetic doesn't improve this year, I'll get left back."

"All right. And if you weren't on a discount, how would you get promoted?" I wondered.

And then Alexis told me about the things that happened in Mr. Karanasis' school. He had been there since the first grade, and knew. Any child who paid full tuition was never left back, even if he was a moron. Whoever was there on a discount was in danger the minute his marks were just a little bit off. Alexis pronounced the words "in danger" in such a way, emphasizing each syllable separately, that I was alarmed.

"We're on a discount, too," I admitted.

"We?"

"My sister and I. She's in the upper classes. But she doesn't have anything to worry about. She's a very good student. She even knows how many stamens an apple blossom has."

"What a show-off you are!"

I was about to answer him back, but just then the bell rang for us to go back to class.

The lesson had hardly begun when Mr. Karanasis came into the classroom again. This time he had Pipitsa's mother with him. Pipitsa's mother started trying out all the desks, one by one, to determine which one wasn't in a draft and which had the best view of the blackboard, so that Pipitsa could sit there. Fortunately, they didn't put her next to me. Not that I was so wild about sitting with Alexis, but he was a lot better than Pipitsa.

Alexis jerked his head in Pipitsa's direction. "Full tuition!" he whispered to me.

"I just love our school!" Myrto said at midday, when we were all seated at the table.

"I don't like that school one bit," I said. "The only thing that looks good is our teacher."

Myrto was enthusiastic because they had hardly had any lesson at all. They chose five or six children from the upper classes, and Mr. Karanasis gave them a talk about how the honor must fall to the lot of our school to organize one of the first Legions of the Youth Organization set up by our dictator. They would be the first Legionnaires, the core of the organization.

"Did he tell you that it was compulsory?" Grandfather asked.

"No. Whoever wants to can join. But if we join now, they'll make us leaders, with three gold stars. Like these."

Myrto opened her fist. Inside it she had three stars that shone like real gold.

"Where did you get them?" Mama wanted to know.

"At Mrs. Angeliki's store."

The truth was that Myrto loved anything that glittered. She had a whole box with gold pen points, and woe unto you if you didn't have anything to write with and you asked her for one. Whenever they gave us money to spend on whatever we liked, Myrto would always go to Mrs. Angeliki's notions store and buy anything she could find that was gold.

"Since it isn't compulsory," Grandfather said gravely, "you will merely bide your time and let the honor of being first fall to the others. I hope that your father is of the same opinion."

"You'll only join later," Papa agreed. "If it's compulsory."

"Then all the others will have been made leaders and I'll never be!" Myrto wailed.

"Why must you discourage the child's initiative?" Great aunt Despina broke in.

But Grandfather cut her short, just as he had that day when the dictatorship came into power.

"You're talking foolishness, Despina!"

That night Myrto put her three stars under her pillow and said, weeping, "Li-po, li-po!"

We came home from school one day to find Manoli having a lesson with our Grandfather.

"Artemis will show up, too," I told Myrto. "Just wait and see."

We plumped ourselves down and got through our homework as fast as we could. And almost before we had finished, there was Artemis.

"Did you come to learn how to sew?" we asked, teasing.

"Not on your life. But I just wasn't going to sit on a rock in Lamagari and let Master Manoli come to see you by himself," she protested.

Great-aunt Despina had gone marketing, so Stamatina opened the parlor door for us so that Artemis could see the wildcat. She didn't even give it a glance. She stared at the chandelier that hung from the middle of the ceiling, stretched out her hand to finger the velvet armchairs, and then went wild looking at herself in the big mirror with the gold frame.

"Why, hello there, my darling sweet Artemis!" she called out to her reflection in the mirror, curtsying one minute and dancing the next.

"It's the first time I've ever seen myself whole," she called out to us while she waltzed around the room.

Tears welled in Stamatina's eyes as she watched her. "The poor little chick, the poor little chick!" she exclaimed. "She's never seen herself in the mirror before."

"Not really," said Artemis, laughing. "I look at my face all the time. My father brought me a pocket mirror. But I never knew how lovely it could be to see your whole self. My dear, it's like the cinema. I saw it last year once in town, and it was marvelous the way those pictures jump around, just like real people!"

In the end she looked at the wildcat, too.

"It looks alive!" she exclaimed.

Artemis couldn't drag herself out of the parlor. She told us that now whenever she heard in fairy stories about kings' palaces she'd know that they looked just like our parlor. If only Great-aunt Despina, who was always grumbling that the furniture had to be changed, could have heard her! The velvet on the armchairs was already worn down to the backing and the braid had come off in places. The sofa springs had gone slack; and the buffet and the console table, after all those years, were full of tiny holes from the worms that eat wood.

Manoli, meanwhile, had finished his lesson and was in a hurry to leave so that he would reach Lamagari before dark. The only way to get there overland was by way of a primitive path, all rough and rocky.

"Wait a while, we'll go together with the boat," Artemis told him. "My father's coming soon to take me."

"And what about the sewing?" Stamatina asked her. "Their aunt isn't back yet." Then she asked her, "Why don't you come too and learn to read and write, along with Manoli?"

"Because if I do, that hut of ours and Lamagari won't be able to hold me any more!"

Sometimes Artemis talked in such a grown-up way that you forgot she was a child, like us.

Manoli and Artemis told us the news of Lamagari. It was already five days since three strangers had come to live there. They were political prisoners, exiles, sent from Athens. The police brought them over one day, and they rented a tiny room in Manoli's hut.

"They're freedom fighters, anti-Fascists," Manoli said, scrutinizing me as though he were asking me if I had kept his secret.

"What do you mean? They're Bolsheviks. That's what Pandeli, the policeman, said," Artemis exclaimed. "If you hold up a crucifix in front of them, he says, they'll drop dead."

"Don't say such stupid things!" Manoli said angrily.

My thoughts flew to Niko. We didn't even know if he was in the town. Maybe Stamatina knew something, but if I were to ask her she would only have answered once again with Great-aunt Despina's words: "The wildcat and Niko are forbidden subjects!"

For three days Alexis was absent from school, and Miss Irene told me to go to his house and ask if he was ill.

Maybe, I thought, he was staying home with his father. A few days before he had told me that his father had arrived from Athens. He used to work there, but now he was going to stay with them on the island.

Alexis' house was two streets beyond ours. I went that far with him once when he had to give me a book, but he hadn't let me come inside. I waited out on the sidewalk. And when he brought me the book he said, "Would you like me to show you our cat? It's an Angora."

I wanted to see it. And I thought he would ask me to come inside. But he disappeared through the door again while I waited once more out on the street. He came back right away, but he didn't have the cat with him.

"I couldn't find her," he said. "I'll show her to you some other time."

And so, when I rang the bell today my heart was beating fast and I wondered if perhaps Alexis himself would come out with his pallid face and stare at me and say, "What are you doing here, at my door?"

But it was his mother who opened the door. She had come to school once to get him and I had seen her then. She wore an old dress, and over it a worn-out flowered apron. She looked at me curiously, as though to ask what I wanted.

"Our teacher, Miss Irene, sent me," I managed to say. "I came to ask if Alexis was sick."

"Come inside and see him." She smiled and moved out of the doorway. I stood there not knowing what to do.

"Come along with me," Alexis' mother said, and took me by the hand.

We went down some stairs and along a very lengthy corridor where there was hardly room to move, because left and right on the floor boards were piles of books that reached almost to the ceiling. Alexis' mother opened a door and we entered a room. There were books there too: books everywhere, on the bare floor, on a trunk, on shelves, and even on the window sill.

Then, for the first time. I caught sight of Alexis' father. He was sitting at a table, writing. He had lit the lamp, in spite of the fact that, outside, there was bright sunshine. Not a ray of light came through the window because they lived in the basement.

"Dimitri," said Alexis' mother, " a little girl from Alexis' class is here. The teacher sent her to ask——"

He raised his eyes to look at me; and then, suddenly, I realized that he was a writer. A writer!

When the children at school asked Alexis, "What does your father do?" he would reply, "Nothing. He writes."

It had not occurred to me then that he might be a writer. But now I could see that he was. He was very pale, like Alexis. And although he didn't have long hair, and was writing with a fountain pen instead of a quill (like the painting I had seen once in one of Grandfather's books), I knew that for the first time in my life I was looking at a writer. I stared as though I had been turned to marble. He didn't say anything; and, I don't know why, I began to feel afraid of him. And I told myself that I would never become a writer!

"The little girl seems to be frightened of you," Alexis' mother said, smiling. Then he smiled, too. His eyes suddenly came to life and became very merry, and all around them his face was filled with fine little wrinkles.

"Are you the one whose name is Melissa?" he asked.

"Yes," I said, feeling encouraged. I was glad Alexis had told him about me.

On a couch, under a blanket, something stirred. I had not noticed Alexis curled up there with his face buried in the pillows.

"Is he sick?" I asked.

Alexis did not budge. His mother went over to him.

"Aren't you going to speak to Melissa?"

His father began telling him a whole lot of things, and I couldn't understand what any of it was about. He said that he ought to be proud that he didn't have new shoes, and that Mr. Karanasis ought to be ashamed because he had told him, "Don't let me see you again with those shabby wrecks on your feet!" And he went on to say that he had left Athens and resigned from the newspaper where he worked because he was not able to write what they wanted him to, and he preferred to have his whole family go barefoot.

He talked in a very loud voice. Alexis' mother got up and shut the door of the room.

"Not so loud, Dimitri. They'll hear you," she said, and began crying.

I started telling myself all over again that I would never become a writer. And then, suddenly, I understood: Alexis hadn't gone to school because his shoes were worn out. It was then that I remembered Myrto's tortures. Myrto had begged and implored them to buy her

some shoes with laces, just like boys'. Great-aunt Despina
went and bought them for her.

And the very first day that Myrto put them on, they
were too tight. She said, "Swear to me that you won't tell
anything to anybody!"

I gave my word.

And so she only wore them once in a while, so that
Mama wouldn't ask her what was wrong, since she had
wanted them so desperately. Whenever she put them on
she would say, "I might as well wear my tortures today."

I was about to tell them the whole story and ask what
size shoe Alexis wore, but his mother kept on crying and
Alexis didn't stir but kept his face pressed into the pillows.

"Well, so your name is Melissa." His father broke the
silence, and his eyes turned merry again and the tiny
wrinkles reappeared all around them.

I told him how my grandfather had named me that
after my grandmother and after an ancient queen.

"And how do you feel about kings and queens?" Alexis'
father asked me.

I was seized by a fit of talking. I told everything; about
Great-aunt Despina and Myrto, who simply loved kings;
and about Grandfather and myself, who didn't want to
have them around at all. I told him about Papa, who was
afraid of losing his position when the dictatorship came
and made us change our cat's name. I told about Myrto
and her stars, how they wanted to make her a leader and
Grandfather said, "Since it's not compulsory, she can just
bide her time." I talked about the wildcat in the glass

case, about Artemis who had declared that our parlor with its shabby velvet armchairs was like a king's palace out of a fairy tale. I started to say, "Our cousin Niko—", but I stopped short and stared down at the floor.

Alexis had raised his head from the pillows, and, propped up on his elbows, was listening from the couch. His mother had stopped crying. In fact, she had even begun to smile. And his father threw back his head and laughed.

"What size shoe do you wear, Alexis?" I quickly changed the subject and began talking about Myrto's tortures.

His father jumped up and kissed me on both cheeks. Then he turned serious. "Perhaps it's my fault, Melissa, for questioning you about kings, but you shouldn't really tell such things to strangers."

"Do you think Papa will lose his job at the bank?" I asked him, terrified.

"Don't worry," he said. "Nothing bad will happen. We are your friends. But you must never talk in front of strangers."

"Don't they look like girls' shoes?" It was Alexis, speaking for the first time.

"Not a bit," I reassured him. "They're exactly like boys'."

"For a few days, then, if your mother doesn't mind," Alexis' mother said. "After that we'll be able to get him new ones."

I said that Mama would be delighted because she didn't think they were at all suitable for a girl. As for Myrto—it was only her gold pen points that she wouldn't give to anyone, and her stars. Everything else she didn't mind at all giving away.

"Your sister: is she the one who knows how many stamens an apple blossom has?" asked Alexis' father, chuckling.

That Alexis! He must have told him everything!

Alexis put on his old wrecks in order to come along and get Myrto's tortures, so as not to miss school the next day.

"I won't go inside your house," he told me. "I'm ashamed. I'll wait in the street."

All the time, while we were on the way to my house, he kept saying, "You'll tell your sister that it's only for three days. After that, they'll get me mine."

I'm sure that I'd rather, a thousand times, wear his old wrecks than beg for stranger's shoes, but Mr. Karanasis had said that it was a disgrace to the whole school for Alexis to wear such shoes. I didn't understand that at all.

"What did you think of my father? Isn't he great?" Alexis asked me when we were almost at my house.

"He's all right," I told him.

But inside myself, I still wasn't sure if I wanted to become a writer.

In bed, at night, I told Myrto all about Alexis' house.

"His father's a real writer. His desk is full of books and dust. He wears a jacket with holes in the elbows and he needs lamp light to write by, even though the sun is shining outside."

"I wouldn't want to have a writer for a father," Myrto said. "Then we might also have to go chasing around the neighborhood begging for borrowed shoes."

I didn't answer her because I didn't know what to say. I remembered how much I had enjoyed the way Alexis' father had spoken to me—as though we had been two friends.

"Ev-po, ev-po!" I called out to Myrto.

For the first time in my life I had seen a real writer, and that was why I was "ev-po."

"Li-po, li-po!" Myrto answered. "Today I told Mr. Karanasis that I wouldn't be the first girl Legionnaire. And now I've lost my chance and I won't be a leader, ever."

⌸ 2 ⌸

Thrift, and Mrs. Angeliki's
Notions Store.

⌸ That fall we no longer went down to the parlor every Thursday, as we had in former years, to Great-aunt Despina's callers. Grandfather and Papa had decided that it was best that we didn't.

"They're only children," they said. "There's no knowing what they might let slip."

But the callers no longer came regularly, as they used to: once a month, sometimes not even as often as that. Great-aunt Despina said bitterly that it was all because of *them*. Niko and the wildcat, I suppose she meant. And so we didn't lay eyes on the wildcat any more, except once in a while when Stamatina remembered to call us in when she was doing the parlor. And that was why I thought it was strange when she called me to her one day when nobody else was around and said, "Would you like to see the wildcat? I have the key to the case."

Three whole days hadn't passed since she had washed

down the panes of the glass case and let us go into the parlor to watch.

"Just a minute and I'll call Myrto."

But Stamatina did not let me call Myrto. She said Myrto was upstairs with Great-aunt Despina. "And I'm in a hurry," she added. "I'll just open it for you for a second so you can see it."

She opened the case. It was all I could do not to cry out. In its teeth the wildcat held a slip of white paper, just as before! My hand shook when I put it between the wildcat's jaws to draw the paper out—not because I was afraid of the teeth, but because I was so impatient to see the message.

AT THREE O'CLOCK TODAY GO AND BUY NOTE-
BOOKS FROM MRS. ANGELIKI'S STORE. GO ALONE.

The Wildcat.

"Look," I said to Stamatina. "'Alone' is underlined two times."

"Then you'll go alone," she said blandly.

"And not even tell Myrto?"

"That's what the paper says," she explained. "Alone."

My heart was beating so fast that I thought it would burst. The time when we got the first message about the half-armed windmill it had been more like a game. But then it had been for all of us, including Manoli, with whom nobody is afraid of anything. I wondered if I ought to wait for when Manoli came for his lesson, so that we could go together. But the message said: *today, alone.*

Mrs. Angeliki's store was in a narrow street behind our

house. You could buy anything there. It didn't only have school supplies, but it also had live birds in gold-painted cages, and chocolates with chances. If, when you unwrapped your chocolate, you found the picture of some rare flower, you could win one of those cages with the bird inside it. Grandfather said that all our thrift, Myrto's and mine, flew straight to Mrs. Angeliki. We weren't very lucky, however, because we had never managed to come across that rare flower.

What, I wondered, would I find now, in Mrs. Angeliki's shop? Would there be, perhaps, a letter from Niko in one of the notebooks that I was going to buy? I didn't like having to go alone, without another child. It wasn't much fun that way.

Mrs. Angeliki knew that I loved the birds. She often let me tap the bars of their cages and they would come and peck at my finger. As soon as I asked for notebooks, she smiled and said, "Come. I want to show you a new bird."

She led me to a tiny door in the back of her shop. She opened it and nodded to me to go inside.

"Melissa!"

Someone spoke. Someone who called me Melissa because I had already grown up. My eyes, still dazzled by the sunlight outside, could hardly make anything out in the half-darkened little room. But before I had grown used to the darkness, two hands picked me up and lifted me into the air.

"Ah, little thrush, little thrush! You're no more than a handful of feathers. Can't you manage to put a few ounces of meat on your bones?"

I was too breathless to speak. What could Niko be doing in Mrs. Angeliki's notions store?

"You see, I haven't gone off yet," he said, and smiled—I could make him out now—as though it were the most natural thing in the world for him to be right there, in the dark little room, among the empty boxes and the piles of notebooks and cages.

He began to ask me about everyone at home, and about Artemis and Manoli. But more than anything else he wanted to learn about those exiles who were living in Manoli's shack.

"Can you keep a secret that only you and Manoli will know?" Niko asked, looking gravely into my eyes.

Of course I could, but it was going to be very hard to have still another secret from Myrto. It was enough that I already had Manoli's. And I wasn't in Lamagari now, where I could dash to the beach whenever I wanted to, and hollow out holes in the sand and call down my secrets into them.

"I can't even tell Myrto?"

"You can't tell anybody," Niko said, looking even more grave.

I gave my word with a heavy heart. Niko took a packet of cigarettes from his pocket, unstuck the seal, opened it, and slid a piece of folded paper under the layer of tin foil. Then he sealed it again.

"Manoli must give it to the exiles," he said, hiding the cigarette box in my pocket. "As soon as he brings it back, you will wait until the wildcat has another message for you, telling you to come here again to buy a notebook. I know this is no game for children," he went on, "but we are living in difficult times."

After that he asked me to tell him all about our school. And once again he was like the old Niko who sang songs and played carefree childish games with us that you didn't have to hide from anyone. I told him everything: about the school, about Alexis and his father.

Niko grew very sad when I told him that Myrto wanted to be a leader in the Youth Organization. He didn't let me say any more because they might start worrying at home about my being away so long.

"Are you going to stay on the island much longer?" I asked him.

"It all depends," he replied, hurriedly stroking my hair.

When I got home, I found them all topsy-turvy. Only Myrto's eyes shone with triumph. She was going to be a leader after all. That was what Papa said. He had come home from his office and announced that his director, Mr. Pericles, had mentioned it to him at the request of Mr. Karanasis, who had complained that Papa would not permit Myrto to become one of the first girl Legionnaires on our island. Papa had explained that she was still young. When she was ready for high school, perhaps . . . Then Mr. Pericles informed him that Mr. Karanasis had chosen her, even though she was so young, because she was so tall and was the prettiest girl in the school. They wanted to make a Legionnaire's uniform for her so that they could take her photograph and send it to magazines all over the world to put on their covers.

Mr. Pericles said that Papa would get a promotion.
Whereas if he didn't permit Myrto—well, he wasn't sure,
but it might have consequences in his job.

"That's all we need," Grandfather said, beside himself.
"To see a child of ours plastered all over the Fascist
magazines. It's a disgrace."

"Just the idea of it is awful," Mama put in, and burst
into tears.

"But I'll lose my job! Don't you understand?" Papa
shouted. "Mr. Pericles made it absolutely clear. There
will be *consequences*. And, in any case, it won't be long
before it will be compulsory, and all the children will
have to join."

"At least let us not be ridiculous enough to be among
the first," Grandfather said furiously.

When Great-aunt Despina started to speak, saying all
over again that they would regret it if they hindered
Myrto from enjoying such a marvelous stroke of luck, we
were sent off to our room. We could hear their voices all
the way upstairs, worse than us children quarreling over
who would be first in Pipitsa's barrel. Before the dictatorship came, no one had ever shouted to anyone else in that
way.

"Did you hear how I'll be in all the magazines?" Myrto
gloated. You'd think she had already made her appear-
ance in them. "And they're going to make me a uniform!"

And I couldn't tell her that I'd seen Niko, and that he
didn't like it, not one bit, her wanting to become a
leader.

"My congratulations," Stamatina said, entering the

room. "You'll be a leader, Madam Myrto. Your father has decided." Then she muttered in a temper, "I wish they'd cut the legs off the frog that's on our backs!"

"Ev-po, ev-po!" Myrto crowed. "Ev-po. I'm going to be a leader!" And, in her jubilation, she kicked her blankets high into the air.

"Li-po, li-po," I murmured, and wrapped myself in my blankets, head and all.

"Li-po," because I had secrets from Myrto. "Li-po," because in our house the grown-ups were all shouting at each other. "Li-po," because Niko was hiding in a dusty little room. "Li-po," because it was now five days that Alexis had been coming to school with borrowed shoes.

We didn't have any lessons on the thirtieth of October because we had to observe "Thrift Day." Grandfather was beside himself.

"It's not enough," he said, "that we have so many saints that you have holidays all the time. Now they have even added Thrift!"

There was going to be a celebration at school on that day. A week earlier, Mr. Karanasis gave us a long lecture about thrift. I couldn't remember much of what he said because Alexis and I were playing tick-tack-toe, and he beat me every time. Thrift, however, meant hiding money. We all had to write compositions and the best ones were going to be read aloud on the day of the celebration.

Naturally, I didn't expect them to read my composition. Miss Irene always marked my themes "Excellent," but this time I couldn't think of anything to write. And I could see Alexis, next to me, frowning and muttering at the blank paper in front of him. What could you say about thrift? All the same, I didn't expect Alexis and me to get zeroes. Mr. Karanasis himself marked the papers.

"Whatever came over you two to make you write like that?" Miss Irene said sadly as she returned our notebooks. "Why didn't you ask me first?"

"Absurd reflections, devoid of content," Mr. Karanasis had inscribed in red ink across the top of my composition. And on Alexis' he had written exactly the same thing.

Alexis had written about an uncle of his who was very rich and who kept all his money stashed away in boxes. He never spent a penny, he dressed in rags, and in the end all his hidden money was gnawed to shreds by the mice. I wrote about a girl who, whenever they gave her money to buy chocolates, hid the money. And when she grew up she never tasted chocolate as long as she lived.

Myrto's was marked "Excellent," and they were going to read her composition at the celebration. It was the best one in the whole school.

I said to her, "But you never hide a single penny, and you're always buying pen points and a whole bunch of shiny gold stuff from Mrs. Angeliki! How could you write that 'the man who practices thrift performs a service to himself and to the community'?"

"I wrote exactly what Mr. Karanasis told us," she replied. "Not like you and Alexis. You've become the laughingstocks of the whole school."

"Do you know what my father said?" Alexis said to me the next day. "He said if he was in Mr. Karanasis' place he would have marked us 'Excellent.' "

The curious thing was that my grandfather had said that he himself would have done the same thing.

"If we had a single coffee cup in our house that didn't have a broken handle," Alexis confided in me, "we'd invite your grandfather to come and see us. My father would like to meet him."

I assured him that Grandfather didn't pay any attention whatever to that sort of thing, and that on his desk he kept a thick cup with a broken handle to drink his coffee out of. He said he couldn't really enjoy it out of any other.

"I will speak to my mother, then," Alexis said gravely.

But before the invitation came, Grandfather and Alexis' father had gotten to know each other in a different fashion.

The sea and the sky were like a single curtain of dark gray. You couldn't make out where one ended and the other began. Vast white waves dashed up on the jetties and broke against them.

"Artemis won't come today," I told Myrto, who was sitting with me in the glass-enclosed porch. We watched the frothing sea.

"Manoli won't come either," I continued as I stared at the rain which had already begun to beat on the glass panes. I was thinking about Niko, waiting in vain for the cigarette packet to come back from Lamagari. Without my even realizing it, I said aloud, "It's too bad." It just slipped out, in spite of me.

"What's too bad?" Myrto asked.

"That Manoli and Artemis won't be able to come."

"I do-on't ca-are!" she sang out. "Now that I'm going to be a Legionnaire, I'm only going to go around with the others in the Legion. Mr. Karanasis said that from now on our friends and brothers and sisters have to be the other Legionnaires."

"And will you care more for those—what did you call them?—Legionnaires of yours more than me?" I asked anxiously.

"Perha-a-a-aps!" Myrto sang out, with trills.

The rain was coming down in buckets, and the lightning flashes cracked across the sky to become lost in the sea that foamed and swelled more and more violently. There was nothing there to recall the serene blue summer water of Lamagari.

"Look!" Myrto exclaimed. "There's someone out there, running in the rain!"

A boy wrapped in an old sack was splashing his way toward the door of our house. It couldn't have been anyone but Manoli. Even before I heard the doorbell ring, I dashed to the stairs and leaped down the steps two by two. Stamatina had already opened the door for him and was crossing herself. What a sight Manoli was: drenched to the bone. Water poured from every part of him. The only thing that was dry was his shoes, because he had taken them off and had kept them tucked under his armpits all the way.

"You could do without so much reading and writing,"

Stamatina grumbled at him. "If you caught pneumonia your poor mother would go out of her mind."

She yanked him into the kitchen and trotted off to find something for him to put on until his own clothes could dry out.

"Look!" Manoli said, when Stamatina had left us. "I didn't get a single drop on it!" And he showed me Niko's packet of cigarettes.

I did not go to see Niko until the next day, even though Manoli had insisted that I take the cigarettes to him as quickly as I could. The message from the wildcat did not come until the following day, which was just as well, because the rain did not let up and I couldn't say that I was going out to buy a notebook in all that downpour.

The next day was clear and balmy, as though it were spring. I looked out at the sea from the classroom window. It was all serene again. Little boats were drifting across it. The previous day's storm seemed completely forgotten. But Alexis remembered it. He was so sleepy that he sprawled across his desk, and twice I had to give him a shove with my elbow because he was about to drop off to sleep.

"It's on account of the rain yesterday," he told me at recess. "None of us slept a wink in our house, all night long. The hall and the front room were flooded. We had to bail all the water out with buckets."

And once again I thought that I didn't want to become a writer and have to live in a basement, ten steps down.

The minute school let out I ran to Mrs. Angeliki's store

for notebooks. I went into the little back room. I stood there frozen with fear. A man was sitting there, a man with a thick mustache, like a brush.

"Thanks a lot for not recognizing me," he said, laughing. And I recognized Niko's voice.

"What are you masquerading like that for?" I wondered.

"What's the matter?" he teased. "Doesn't it suit me?"

I couldn't get used to it. He seemed like a stranger to me.

I handed him the packet of cigarettes. He withdrew a slip of paper from it and read it. Then he tore up the paper into little pieces, struck a match, and burned them. When I told him how Manoli had brought it in the middle of all the downpour, his face grew sad.

"Would you like me to give you a cage with a canary?" he asked, suddenly changing the subject. "Mrs. Angeliki says you like them."

"And what would I tell them at home?"

"You could say you had a lucky chance."

"Wouldn't that be lying?" I asked, and my heart pounded very hard, because I longed to have the cage with the canary in it. Then, too, Myrto and I always went together to buy the chocolates with the chances, and we always unwrapped them together, and she always told me it was my fault that we hadn't won.

"You're right. It would be lying," Niko said, and it seemed to me that he was sorry that he couldn't give me a canary.

He wouldn't let me leave. He wanted to hear everything that went on at home and at school. When I told

him that Myrto was going to be a Legionnaire on the
fourth of November, when there was going to be a big
celebration at school to mark the end of three months
since the founding of the dictatorship, he did not get
angry at Myrto. It was like the time when he blamed us
for wanting to bury Pipitsa alive. Now he blamed Mr.
Karanasis. He told me that although no other school had
as yet organized a Legion because none of the children
wanted to join, Mr. Karanasis wanted to force the issue
and be the first to establish one.

How could Niko possibly know all that, shut up in the
little room with the cages?

"The wildcat comes and tells me everything," he explained when he saw the astonishment in my face.

I went home with the cigarette packet once more in
my pocket. I loved walking all alone in the narrow streets
of the town. They were so narrow that when you
stretched out both your arms you could almost touch the
houses on both sides. They were cobbled with stones,
sometimes square ones and sometimes rectangular ones.
Pipitsa always said that we mustn't step on the lines that
divided the stones because if we did we would marry an
old man when we grew up. Of course it was just nonsense, but I liked stepping on tiptoes from cobblestone to
cobblestone without touching the lines. And under my
breath I would make a wish.

"I wish we could go to Lamagari with Niko in the
summer!" I said today under my breath. And I reached
home without ever having stepped on a single line.

⊐ 3 ⊐

The Harmful Books, Myrto's Stiff Neck, and the Silliness of Sillinesses.

⊐ Grandfather was perfectly right when he said that all we ever had was holidays. One day, not long after that, we had sat through only two classes when, at recess, Mr. Karanasis made us gather in the schoolyard and told us to form a line.

"You will not be going back to your classrooms," he announced. "Instead, I am going to take you to the town square where the entire school will learn a great and important lesson."

"Do you think he's going to take us on one of those 'Know-your-Community' walks?" I asked Alexis.

"Something else is going on," he answered. "The upper classes are going too. They're too big for that."

When we reached the square, everything was very confusing. Right in the middle, just where the column stood with the marble lion on it, a huge bonfire was blazing. A little beyond it, on a platform, stood the

Mayor, Amstradam Pikipikiram, Pipitsa's father, and the Bishop in his vestments. People stood all around the bonfire, mostly children in groups from the schools. We couldn't figure out what was going on.

Soon two men arrived lugging enormous sacks on their shoulders. They shoved people aside to get through. When they got close to the fire, they emptied their sacks onto it. It was books!

"What are they doing?" Alexis asked a boy who was standing next to us.

"They're burning the harmful books," he told us.

Mr. Karanasis climbed up onto the platform and started to deliver a lecture. He talked about the harmful and dreadful books that poison the soul and make man criminal.

"Let's go nearer and watch," Alexis said.

We wriggled through the crowd and got close to the bonfire. You would have thought it was St. John's Eve, when the children light bonfires to burn the May Day wreaths and jump over them. The children from the upper classes were taking running leaps now. It was curious how the books burned. At first, when the pages caught fire, the book opened as though some invisible hand had touched it. Then, as it burned, it looked like a flower closing its petals. Soon the fire died down and the primary-school children could jump over it.

But the men reappeared with their sacks and emptied them. The flames rose higher and higher. The children shrieked. Hoopla! Who can leap highest? At one moment, while a sack was being dumped out, some of the books landed right at our feet. I started to kick one of them toward the fire. And then I stopped. I had seen that book somewhere before. It had a black binding with gold letters on the cover. I flipped the cover open with the toe of my shoe, and then I was sure. It was one of Grandfather's Ancients. Grandfather had written his signature in purple ink in all his books. I knew it at once, thick and broad, on the flyleaf. Grandfather never let anybody touch his books. How had his Ancient gotten here, ready to fall into the fire? I stooped and picked it up. For a moment I held it in my hand.

"Well, throw it!" Alexis whispered to me. He grabbed the book from my grasp and flung it into the fire. "Can't you see they're watching you?"

I grew confused. From the platform, Mr. Karanasis and Pikipikiram were looking in my direction and saying something. I glanced around me. I could see children yelling, and even grown-ups, too, and leaping over the fire. Most of the people, however, just stood there silently, their lips pressed together. I scanned their faces one by one, certain that I would find a man with his hat brim pulled down so that it nearly hid his eyes, and with a thick mustache, like a brush.

Then, without even knowing why I was doing it, I started to push my way past the other children in order to back out of the ever-tightening circle which was drawing Alexis and me, standing in the front row as we were, ever closer to the bonfire. Alexis was behind me. We stood a little way beyond the crowd and caught our breath. In the air above our heads bits of charred paper flew about like bats.

"You should have seen the look Mr. Karanasis gave you when you bent over to pick up that book!" Alexis said.

When the fire went out and they didn't have any more books to throw on it, the crowd began to break up. Mr. Karanasis said that it was too late for us to go back to school, and dismissed us. Alexis and I set off for home. I don't know why, but I had not yet told him that the book I had stooped to pick up was one of Grandfather's Ancients. When we were out of the square, I noticed Grandfather standing near the wall of a house. Alexis' father stood beside him. They did not know each other. They stood almost back to back, not speaking. Grandfather was poking with his cane at the burned paper which filled the street and the sidewalk. Alexis and I ran toward them.

"Grandfather, one of your Ancients got into the fire!" I said.

Grandfather nodded his head. "I know."

Alexis' father turned around in surprise.

"Well, Melissa, introduce me to your grandfather."

"Grandfather, this is Alexis' father——"

The two of them were shaking hands even before I could finish.

"Did they take some of your books?" Alexis' father asked in a low voice.

"They came this morning with their sacks," my grandfather replied.

Glancing around him, Alexis' father said, "They took my manuscripts as well."

Alexis and I went on ahead while Grandfather and

Alexis' father followed. There was a gust of wind and the bits of charred paper whirled in the middle of the road as though they were dancing.

"Our island will not forget the shame of this day," I heard my grandfather say.

"I'm afraid that this is only the beginning," came the voice of Alexis' father.

"Look!" Alexis said, pointing to the papers. They had swirled into the shape of a large "O."

Plato! The word had an "o" and it was the name of Grandfather's Ancient that had been burned in the bonfire.

When I first learned the alphabet, I fell in love with the letter "o." I was jealous of Myrto because her name was spelled with an "o." When I learned to make syllables, I would go to Grandfather's bookcase and he let me climb the little stepladder and read out the names on the covers of his Ancients. "Pla-to. Plato."

"Grandfather, can I name my teddy bear that?" I had asked him.

Grandfather had chuckled. "If he's a wise philosopher, like Plato."

He wasn't, of course. But I liked the name Plato and that was what I christened him.

When we returned home, Grandfather took me into his study. On the shelves the empty holes gaped where the missing books had stood.

"What you saw today, Melissa, is something you must never forget as long as you live. And after I am dead I want the places where the books were to remain empty, just to remind you."

That's what my grandfather said. And for the first time in my life, from the time I was born, I suppose, I saw him sit with his back hunched, and not straight up, as he always had.

Myrto had not been in the square to see the bonfire because she had been sent to try on her Legionnaire's uniform.

"Li-po, li-po," she said before we fell asleep. "Because I missed the bonfire."

"Li-po, li-po," I said. "Because I saw the bonfire."

I closed my eyes but sleep wouldn't come. Now I saw Niko with that mustache like a brush. Then I saw an "O" roll along in the middle of the street. And fire, fire, fire! The flames stretched up to lick at Grandfather's bookcase and get at his wise books.

Since the day of the bonfire, as soon as I heard Grandfather's "Pa, vou, ga, de, ke, zo, ni," I knew that soon the doorbell would ring, and it would be Alexis' father. He and Grandfather had become friends.

Every day when we came home from school Granfather asked us, "Well, what did you do today?"

We told him what lessons we had had, and if we had learned anything new. The last time Myrto answered, "I didn't have any lessons. Mr. Karanasis called me out of the class for a rehearsal."

Grandfather shook his head. "That's a fine way to learn how to read and write."

To tell the truth, there weren't regular lessons in my class either. They were always summoning some child for a rehearsal, because the big celebration of "the anniversary of our dictatorship and our good fortune," as Mr. Karanasis called it, was drawing near.

"Did you notice," Alexis said to me, "how the 'regulars' are going to recite the longest poems, while to us, the discount children, they only give a few lines?"

I hadn't noticed. I had only been astonished that Pipitsa, who recited worse than anybody in the entire class, was going to have such a long poem. She said the whole thing in one breath, without any commas or periods, in that monotonous whining voice of hers. Poor Miss Irene's face broke out in a sweat when she tried to convey to Pipitsa some understanding of what she was saying. But it was no use.

There was a girl named Antigone in our class. When Miss Irene called on her to recite a poem you couldn't even hear anyone breathe in the room. Antigone was neither a "regular" nor a discount pupil. She was "gratis." Her mother worked as a servant in Mr. Karanasis' house. Instead of paying her a salary, he let Antigone go to his school. Alexis and I felt sorry for her. We thought that really it was better to be a discount pupil than "gratis." Whatever mischief the other children got into, Antigone was punished for it. If they messed up the toilets or splattered ink on the walls, Mr. Karanasis came along and called her out of the classroom to go and clean it up. She didn't share her desk with anyone. The number of children in our class wasn't even, and someone had to sit alone. And Mr. Karanasis reproved our teacher for putting Antigone next to Amstradam Pikipikiram's daughter.

"It is high time, Miss Irene," he told her, "that you learned to distinguish the wheat from the chaff."

She blushed like a poppy. So did Antigone. She stuffed her books into her schoolbag and moved over to the single desk, biting her lips so as not to cry. Little Pikipikiram burst out sobbing. She was a nice little girl, very stubby and as pale as writing paper. She wasn't a good student and at recess time she would beg Antigone, "Will you let me peek in spelling?"

Antigone let her. She also lent her notebooks to copy out the exercises. She even helped her in drawing so that she got marked "Excellent," whereas by herself the poor thing couldn't manage to draw a straight line.

Every night now, before we fell asleep, Myrto memorized the oration she was going to recite at the celebration. Alexis called Myrto's speech "the silliness of sillinesses." Mr. Karanasis himself had written it for her.

The night before the celebration, Myrto wanted to rehearse it once more. She stood up in her bed, pulled the pillowcase off the pillow, put her foot on it, and began to recite.

"I trample you underfoot, odious banner of the enemy! And I bare my breast to the inimical saber. And even though I fall, staining the earth with my heart's blood——"

At this point Myrto stretched herself out prone on the bed, clenched the pillowcase between her teeth, and went on, "—I rend you with my teeth until my last breath is expended . . ."

"What are you doing?" I cried. "You're ripping the pillowcase!"

She was so annoyed at my interrupting her that, with a

single bound, she leaped onto my bed. The bedspring was jolted out of position and, before I knew what had happened, the two of us were on the floor. Myrto held on to the bed rails, howling that she had sprained her neck. At the same instant our grandfather, Papa, Mama, Great-aunt Despina, and Stamatina burst into the room, all demanding at the same time to know what had happened. Myrto screeched in a panic that she couldn't turn her head. Papa said they ought to massage it. Mama said no, that wasn't right, they would have to rub salve onto it. Great-aunt Despina clasped her to her bosom. And Stamatina set to work to put the bed together again.

In the morning Myrto woke up with a stiff neck. She looked as though her head had not been quite screwed on all the way, and she could only look on the right side.

"How am I ever going to give my speech?" she wailed. "How am I ever going to become a Legionnaire?"

Mama, Stamatina, and Great-aunt Despina combined forces and managed to get her dressed. It wasn't an easy job. I felt sorry for poor Myrto, but even so, she was still a terribly comical sight.

We went to school along with Great-aunt Despina and Mama. Myrto implored Grandfather to come and see her recite in her Legionnaire's outfit, but he refused. "It is one opportunity I prefer to pass up," he said.

We reached the school and entered the large assembly room where the program was going to take place. Alexis was there too, with his mother. He had on Myrto's tortures, and his mother was wearing the same faded blue dress she had worn all the other times I had seen her. The program began. The first speech was made by Mr.

Karanasis. While it went on, Alexis and I found a splendid game to play. In front of us sat some child's mother. She had on a dress with little squares printed all over it. Each square had a different design: a camel, a date palm, or a monkey. Each of us asked the other in turn, "In ten little squares, how many—say—camels?" The one who guessed the right number won.

We didn't even realize that Mr. Karanasis had concluded. He must even have said "Long live the King! Long live our Leader! Long live the Nation!" because the children were shouting back so loudly that I could hardly hear Alexis, who was saying to me, "Three monkeys in six squares!"

Then the gym teacher gave a loud beat on a drum. Mr. Karanasis stood in the middle of the platform and said, "I am now going to introduce our island's first Legionnaires. We have the great honor of their being from our school."

Through the doors behind the platform marched six children, three boys and three girls. They were dressed in dark blue uniforms with white ties and forage caps. Some had two stars; others, three, on their shoulders. They stood at attention and saluted with their arms stretched straight out and high in front of them. Alexis said that was the Fascist salute. Only one girl wasn't looking straight ahead as she should have. Her head was twisted to the right, as though it hadn't been screwed on properly. It was my sister Myrto. She looked so funny that Alexis and I couldn't hold back our laughter. Suddenly Alexis stopped laughing and jabbed me with his elbow.

"Look, look!" he said. "It's Koskoris!"

Right beside Myrto stood a short stout boy with

slicked-back hair. It was Koskoris, who was always making trouble in school. Once they caught him smoking in class. He stole pencils and erasers from the other children, and was always fighting. Mr. Karanasis told him, every time, "If you do it again, I'll expel you." But he never punished him. Alexis said that Koskoris not only paid regular tuition, but that his father was connected with the police.

I turned around to see Mama, who was sitting further back. She had bent her head so as to avoid having to look at Myrto. But Great-aunt Despina sat very stiffly upright, looking proud.

When Myrto went up to the platform to speak her piece, Mr. Karanasis announced: "And now, our girl Legionnaire will recite an oration written by my humble self, entitled 'The Bolsheviks Must Die!'"

Lying on the floor of the platform was a red flag which Myrto was supposed to trample and rend with her teeth. It was placed to the left of her, and when she started trampling it her twisted head was turned to the right. When the time came for her to lie down, I saw her propping herself on her arms and legs, with her body in the air.

"The other children had messed up the floor so much with their feet that I would have gotten my uniform dirty if I'd lain down," she told me later, when I asked her why she had gotten herself into such an awkward position.

When she finished the silliness of sillinesses, Mr. Karanasis took her by the hand and they took a bow together. Alexis laughed so hard that I began to get annoyed. It really was a pity about Myrto.

Once we were home, Mama burst into tears. She cried like a child. It was the first time I had ever seen a grown-up cry. She said that it would have been better for Papa to lose his job and for us to live like the gypsies who camped out in the vacant lot behind our house, rather than have Myrto become a Legionnaire and march beside Koskoris, who was a thief. Papa shouted that she was talking like an infant. Grandfather defended Mama. Great-aunt Despina took Papa's part.

And Myrto, with her head still twisted to one side, stood in front of the big mirror in the parlor, trying to improve her Fascist salute. The wildcat watched her with his black eye blazing, while his blue eye was filled with sadness. I went close to him. I looked to see if there might be a bit of white paper in his jaws. How many days had passed, I wondered, since the last time I had seen Niko?

"If the wildcat doesn't have a message for you, don't come," Niko had told me, "not even if Manoli brings the cigarettes."

I wanted to spend the day there, in a corner of the parlor, beside the wildcat. I didn't want to go anywhere in the rest of the house where the grown-ups were arguing. If only Papa would lose his job, I reflected. It wouldn't be a bad idea at all if we went and lived in the vacant lot like the gypsies. We could have an old bus, just like theirs, for a house; and we could hang little flowered calico curtains at the windows.

149

And when winter was over we would wander from town to town. We might even make our way to the other islands; and even further, to the mainland of Greece. Perhaps we might even reach Athens and see the Acropolis about which Grandfather had told us time and time again. After that we could go to other cities and foreign lands, wandering over the whole wide world. And then maybe Myrto would be just the way she had been before she bought the gold stars from Mrs. Angeliki's store. Now, the only thing that was left from the old days was our asking each other every night, "Li-po? Ev-po?"

"Ev-po! Ev-po!" Myrto always answered.

And I, "Li-po, li-po."

⊒ 4 ⊒

They Kill the Wildcat. Another
Doleful Tale, and Myrto's Feat.

⊒ The days dragged past. Why, I wondered, hadn't Manoli brought a cigarette packet? Why hadn't Niko sent a message? I kept dashing over to Mrs. Angeliki's store to buy something. Each time, I told myself, she would say, "Would you like to look at a strange bird?"

But she stayed silent. Stamatina stayed silent too. And the wildcat stayed silent as well.

I was convinced then that Niko had gone away.

"Really, where can Niko be?" Myrto asked me suddenly, on a dreary Sunday when we were once more watching the raindrops on the windowpanes. I looked at her in surprise. I thought she had believed that Niko had left long before this.

"He's in Athens," I told her. "Where else could he be?"

"Mr. Karanasis and the leader of our Legion say he's in the town," Myrto told me in a confidential tone. "And he asked me, as a matter of fact, if he has a thick mustache, like a brush. I told him he doesn't have any mustache and that he had gone away, because ever since we've been going to school he hasn't sent us any more messages with the wildcat."

"You blabbed about the wildcat?" I said, terrified.

Myrto stood up like a rooster, ready for a fight. "I didn't *blab*, my dear little Melia. Our leader is supposed to know what goes on in our houses. And I am supposed to tell what you do, what Stamatina does, what Grandfather—"

"But Grandfather has told us thousands of times, 'Don't wash your linen in public'! No matter what happens at home, we're not supposed to spread it outside," I cried, unable to hold back my tears. "I'm going to tell Grandfather everything, and Mama and Papa, too!"

"Tattletale!" she shrilled.

"*I'm* a tattletale? What about you, blabbing Niko's secrets when they can do something to harm him?"

"You, you! You're the tattletale," she insisted. "You're the one who wants to tell Grandfather. I only tell my leader. That's because I'm a Legionnaire . . ."

That evening the whole house was in a turmoil. Grandfather shook with rage.

"Who ever heard of such a thing?" he stormed. "Making children spy in their own homes!"

Papa said, "What could I do? What could I do? They would have dismissed me from the bank."

Mama just wept all over again and didn't say anything.

Great-aunt Despina said, "I don't see anything so tragic about it!"

Stamatina shook her head. "It's too late now. They've cast a black spell on the child."

But when Stamatina learned that Myrto had told about the first letter which the wildcat had sent to welcome us home, she turned pale. She bundled herself up in her shawl and said to Mama, "You had better look after the supper, Madam. I have to visit my cousin who is sick."

She dashed out into the street, even though the rain was pelting down in torrents.

The next morning, when Papa had left for work and we were getting ready to go to school, there was a loud knocking at the front door. Stamatina opened it and the house filled with policemen. They showed Grandfather a piece of paper and he told them, "You can search as much as you like. You're putting yourself to trouble over nothing. My grandson left last summer."

They weren't interested in searching anywhere except in the parlor, and they asked for the key of the glass case. Great-aunt Despina produced it and started to go into the parlor to open the case, but they wrenched the key out of her hand. "We'll look for ourselves," they said.

We were already late for school. No one had remembered to tell us that we had to leave. Only Myrto glanced for a moment at the clock.

"We'll be late! Come on, Melia," she told me, and began to pick up her schoolbag.

"There will be no school today," Grandfather told her in a tone of absolute finality.

"My leader will be waiting for me after class," Myrto grumbled.

"Let him wait!" Grandfather sounded very angry indeed.

"May I inform him that it was because of you that I couldn't go?"

"You may tell him just that!"

Stamatina had been right in saying that they had cast a spell on Myrto. To talk like that, to Grandfather!

The policemen showed no sign of leaving the parlor. Stamatina went and rapped on the door.

"If you mess up that room, I'll make you tidy it up again!" she called to them.

They opened the door and came out, scowling. Stamatina kept on railing nervously at them.

"Why don't you look in the grandfather's clock? Maybe the person you're searching for crept inside it!"

The policemen went away. Stamatina opened the parlor door, glanced inside, and clapped her hands to her head.

"Holy Mother of God!" she whispered. "Holy Mother of God!"

I ran over to her, and then I stood, petrified, in front of the open door. On the floor in the middle of the parlor the wildcat lay stretched out on its back. Its belly was ripped open and the carpet was littered with straw.

"They killed him, Stamatina!" I cried, and burst into tears.

I went over to it and picked up its head. There, where its blue eye had been, a hole now gaped. Everything was finished now. It would never bring us another message

154

from Niko. And in the summers, at Lamagari, Niko would never be able to tell us any more stories about the wildcat.

"It was always dead anyway. We only believed those stupid stories about it."

It was Myrto who said that. She had come into the room and stood over me. I turned and stared at her. No, this was not my own sister. It was some strange girl that I had seen at the celebration at school marching next to that thief Koskoris and giving the Fascist salute.

Now, throughout the town, they were searching for the man with the mustache like a brush, the one they said looked like Niko. Every day when Stamatina came back from her marketing she told us the news, even before she set down her shopping bag.

"Today they were searching in the neighborhood just beyond ours." . . . "Today they were searching the churches, even behind the altar."

I trembled every time for fear I would hear her say they had been searching in Mrs. Angeliki's store and the little room with the cages. At last, one day, Stamatina blew out her breath in a heavy sigh and said, "It looks as though it's all forgotten now, thank goodness. No one's concerned any more about the man with the mustache like a fat brush. They're positive by now that he really left the town." That was what Stamatina said. And it was true that everything seemed to have quieted down. In the parlor, in the wildcat's case, Great-aunt Despina's good dishes were now arrayed, the ones with the exotic birds painted on them.

"What became of the wildcat?" I asked Stamatina. But

she did not know, and Great-aunt Despina would permit no discussion of the matter. In the house no one mentioned Niko or the wildcat. It had been different before, because I had Myrto to talk things over with. But now all she cared about was her Legion, which hadn't really become a Legion yet because there were still only six Legionnaires in the school, as in the beginning.

"Soon you will all be Legionnaires!" Mr. Karanasis threatened. "It will become compulsory."

One day Alexis was absent from school again. I wondered if something had happened to Myrto's tortures. For days now they had round holes in their soles. Alexis had stuffed them with cardboard and newspaper to keep out the water. He couldn't have been sick, because the previous afternoon when his father came to see Grandfather, he had brought Alexis with him. From the time Alexis' father had begun coming to our house, Grandfather had ordered a lighted brazier to be placed in his study. It wasn't a big one, like Great-aunt Despina's; nor did it have a brass bird on its lid. All the same, it spread a lovely warm glow throughout the whole room. A little pot with water and eucalyptus leaves sat simmering among the ashes, giving out a pungent fragrance. Alexis and I sat there with them because I had wanted to show Alexis one of Grandfather's books with pictures of the *Iliad*. The book was on one of the top shelves. We climbed the stepladder to find it and perched on the steps, leafing through it. I had seen it many times, which is why I merely glanced at it and waited for Alexis to look as long as he liked before turning the page. At one instant I looked down at Grandfather's study. How different it seemed from high up! I could see Grandfather's shiny bald spot. Close beside it was Alexis' father's head of jet-black hair. As they spoke they kept their voices low.

"Just look at the way Achilles is dragging Hector's dead body behind his chariot!" Alexis said, showing me the picture. "I'm on Hector's side," he went on. "What about you, Melissa?"

"I'm for Achilles, naturally, because he's a Greek."

"What difference does that make? The Greeks behaved shamefully to the Trojans."

"Then you're on the side of the enemies of Greece?"

Alexis' father raised his head and looked at us. "Who are these enemies that Alexis is on the side of?"

"He's for the Trojans," I answered. "And he says the Greeks were in the wrong."

Grandfather and Alexis' father laughed.

"The Greeks were in the wrong because they went out to conquer another country," Alexis' father said.

I was genuinely astonished. "But we're Greeks! How can we be on the enemy's side?" I wanted to know.

Then Alexis' father said some very strange things. If, he said, the Greeks wanted to conquer another country, and declared war, we ought to defend that other country and not let it be enslaved.

"It seems pretty confusing, doesn't it, Melia? Never mind. When you grow up you'll understand it better."

I looked at the picture of Hector saying farewell to his wife and child. And after that, I saw him dead, tied to Achilles' chariot and being dragged in the dust.

"It's all *very* confusing," I replied. And they all laughed.

But to get back to Alexis. As I said, he had been absent from school one day. As soon as we were dismissed I ran to his house. There was something very queer about it; the outer door was open.

"Alexis!" I called. "Alexis!"

No one answered. I went inside and looked in all the rooms. No one was there. I found Alexis in the kitchen. He had broken bits of bread into a cup of milk and was eating it very slowly with a spoon. He didn't even notice me standing there in the doorway.

"Are you sick?" I asked.

He raised his head, startled.

"Is school over?" was all he asked.

"Alexis, what's the matter?"

"They arrested my father, Melia . . . the policemen. They came in the night and got him out of bed. They took him in his pajamas. My mother went to find out where they took him. She didn't want me to go with her."

I stood motionless in the doorway. I felt as though I were sinking, as though my heart were sinking into a great sadness. The kitchen was damp and dark. The sink was cracked. And Alexis was eating bread and milk out of a cup with no handle. Grandfather had said that Alexis' father wrote very wise and beautiful books. Then why had the policemen dragged him from the house as though he were a thief? I remembered how they had arrested Odysseus' father the year before, and how his wife and the old grandmother and the children all ran behind him, screaming. But he had been fishing with dynamite, which

158

was against the law. Alexis' father had done nothing bad. He didn't even work. He only wrote books.

No. I was never, never, never going to become a writer, not even to write down the happy and the doleful tales that I thought of! It would be a terrible thing to have them come and get you out of your bed in the middle of the night and drag you through the street in your pajamas; and your pajamas would be gray and red striped ones, like Alexis' father's, with big gray patches on the pants and at the elbows.

"What are they going to do to him, Melia?" Alexis asked suddenly. I felt that he was ready to cry.

"Maybe we had better go and ask my grandfather."

Alexis was absent from school for three days. On the third day he went with his mother to the jail and they waited and waited to be allowed to see his father, but his father was being sent into exile, to another island even further away from Athens than ours, and they wouldn't let anyone see him. The fourth day Alexis came to school. When Miss Irene asked him if he had been sick, he answered "No" so abruptly that she did not say anything else.

As soon as the lesson started, Mr. Karanasis came into the classroom.

"Children of traitors are not allowed to study with the children of good families," was all he said.

We didn't understand what he meant. Then I saw Alexis stuff his books into his bag and walk silently toward the door.

159

"Good-by, my boy," Miss Irene called to him when he was nearly out of the room.

Mr. Karanasis turned and gave her a look, such a look that it made her blush. Then he too went out, slamming the door behind him.

"Why did Alexis go away?" everyone asked.

"I don't know," Miss Irene answered. She picked up the chalk and started writing out the lesson on the blackboard.

"And what is going to happen now, Grandfather?"

"What is going to happen, Melissa?"

"How is the story going to end?"

"What story?"

"Well, Alexis' father is in exile. Alexis left school. Myrto is under a black spell—anyway, that's what Stamatina says. Niko doesn't even write to us. How is the story going to end, Grandfather?"

"I don't know, Melissa. I really don't know."

For the first time I had asked my grandfather something and he had answered that he didn't know. And he said it as though he were very sad that he didn't.

And Sunday came around again, drearier than ever. I wanted to go to Alexis' house, but Papa would not let me. "It would be better," he said, "for Alexis to come here to us." But Alexis did not want to leave his mother all alone, and she never came to our house. Probably, I thought, she was ashamed to go visiting in that faded old blue dress.

I sat in the glass-enclosed porch and longed for those

dreary Sundays of last winter when Myrto and I had been bored together and played "Our Grandfather the Beggar Man" and counted the drops that trickled along the panes. Now, every Sunday afternoon, Myrto went off to her Legion. And whenever Papa threatened not to let her go, her leader told Mr. Karanasis, who told the director of Papa's bank, who called him in and repeated that there would be "consequences." I waited with my nose stuck to the glass to see if Myrto would appear. It grew dark. The lights of the quay started to go on, one by one. She still hadn't returned.

"Hasn't that girl shown up yet?" asked Stamatina, who had come and stood beside me to watch the street.

"She's very late." I had begun to be really worried.

While we were speaking, Grandfather left to go to the school to see what was going on. Mr. Karanasis left one classroom open where the Legionnaires could meet on Sundays.

When he returned, Grandfather announced, "The school is closed tight. There's not a soul inside."

In a little while he put his hat on again and went off to search the streets.

"I said as much! I said as much!" Stamatina cried, wringing her hands in despair. "Something terrible has happened to her, going around with those good-for-nothings in that filthy old Legion!"

Grandfather returned once more. Mama and Papa came home, and Great-aunt Despina returned from her visits. But Myrto was nowhere to be seen. They were all terribly upset. Everyone had a different idea as to what we ought to do.

"We could ask at Koskoris' house," I said at last. "He lives near the school."

"Who's that?" Grandfather asked.

"You remember, Grandfather," I answered. "He's the boy who steals erasers. He's a Legionnaire, along with Myrto."

"You're talking nonsense, Melia!" snapped Great-aunt Despina.

"Go put on your coat, Melissa," Grandfather said. "We'll go together."

I raced up the stairs to our room, to put my coat on. As I opened the door I could hear loud sobs. Face down on her bed, still wearing her shoes, lay Myrto.

"Myrto! Myrtoula! What's the matter?" I cried, and ran over to her.

She didn't answer. She just kept on sobbing, only louder. I didn't know what to do.

"Well, Melia, are you coming?" It was Grandfather's voice from downstairs.

I ran to the stair well and, without going down, I called them all up to our room. They came running. They started asking questions all together and all over again. Every time, whenever anything happens, the grown-ups start asking questions all together and they only get everything more confused.

"What happened?"

"Why were you late?"

"How did you get into the house without our seeing you?"

"Where were you?"

"Who was with you?"

At one moment Stamatina said, "The back door was unlocked."

They all stopped talking. Why, I wondered, should Myrto have entered the house by the back door, like a thief?

Then Grandfather spoke. "Get her something hot to drink, Stamatina, and let's let her sleep. At least she's home and unharmed, and that's the most important thing."

"Do you want me to sit by your bed tonight?" Mama asked.

But Myrto did not move or say a word. She just sobbed and sobbed without stopping. Grandfather made a sign for everyone to leave the room. He said in a low voice, to me, "Perhaps she will talk to you. If you need us, call us. Nobody will be sleeping."

When we were alone in the room, Myrto still did not want to say anything to me. Nor did she say anything the next day. She didn't cry any more. She just lay in her bed and stared at the ceiling. I didn't go to school either because I had hardly slept all night, and in the morning Mama made me go to sleep. I opened my eyes just for a moment and saw Myrto motionless in her bed and everyone coming into the room and going out on tiptoes. Grandfather went to the school to see if he could find out what had happened. He asked Mr. Karanasis. He asked the other Legionnaires. But they all said that absolutely nothing had occurred. The meeting had merely lasted a little longer than usual and they hadn't realized how late it was.

"They are all liars," Grandfather declared, raging,

163

when he came back home. "They say they never budged from the school building, but when I went there I saw it was locked tight."

Myrto slept. She slept for hours at a stretch. The doctor came and gave her an injection. When night fell, Stamatina sent them all off to bed, saying that she would stay and keep watch beside Myrto. She got a chair, set it beside Myrto's bed, and lit a little lamp.

"What do you think happened to her, Stamatina?" I asked in a low voice. "Do you think they really put a spell on her?"

"You go to sleep now," she said. "Tomorrow it will all be over. You'll see."

"Li-po, li-po," I said to myself, pulling the blankets up over my head.

I wasn't sure if I had awakened or if I was still dreaming. But it really must have been a dream. What was Niko doing in our room, sitting beside Myrto's bed? And yet I saw him as plain as anything. The tiny lamp lit up the room and cast his enormous shadow on the ceiling overhead. It was Niko, only he didn't have the thick brushy mustache any more. It couldn't be a dream; I could hear his voice, whispering, but perfectly clear.

"And now, go to sleep," he was telling Myrto. "It was a bad dream and now it's over. Do you see how I kept my promise and came?"

Was it a dream, then? To whom had Niko made a promise to come? To Myrto? But he hadn't laid eyes on her since the time he left Lamagari.

My eyelids were heavy with sleep. It was an effort to lift them. I finally managed to get them open and sat up in bed. I was awake. And the person who was sitting beside Myrto was really Niko.

"Niko," I whispered.

"Are you awake, little one?"

"Is it all over? Are you going to stay home now?"

"Nothing's over, Melissa." Niko's voice sounded sad. "I'm leaving the island tomorrow, and I came to say goodby to you both."

"Well, tell her what happened!"

Myrto had spoken. Her voice was so weak and thin it barely managed to emerge from her throat.

And then Niko told me about Myrto's feat.

Sunday afternoon, at school, their leader told them that every Legionnaire had to perfom a feat. Everyone had to do something for the Legion.

Then he said to Myrto, "It's your turn today."

"What am I supposed to do?" she asked.

"We'll tell you as soon as it gets dark."

"I have to go home as soon as it gets dark. I'll get scolded if I don't."

"Scarecat!" Koskoris mocked her. "They won't scold you. For the Legion's sake you have to be ready to dare everything."

As soon as it was really dark they left the school and made their way through a maze of alleyways until they emerged onto a vacant lot. There was not a soul around, only a lot of miaowing cats, so many that their feet got all tangled up among them.

"Koskoris would have done the feat," the leader said in a whisper, "only he's too big."

"What do I have to do?" Myrto asked again.

"Swear on the honor of the Legion and I'll tell you."

"I swear."

"This lot is at the back wall of Mrs. Angeliki's store," the leader explained, still whispering. "Last night I made the hole bigger."

"What hole?"

"The hole the cats go through."

He removed two big stones from the wall and told Myrto to see if she could squeeze through.

"And what am I supposed to do in the store?" she asked, astonished. "It's shut now."

"You'll look around with this flashlight that we'll give you. You mustn't turn on any lights. And you'll bring us three boxes of whistles with white lanyards, ten scout knives, and as many chocolates—the ones with the chances—as you can carry. The more the better."

"How can I bring them?" Myrto asked, confused. "Mrs. Angeliki won't be there. That's stealing!"

"Stealing?" said the leader angrily. "Bringing things that your Legion needs is stealing? What sort of feat would it be if you went in there in broad daylight, with money, and bought the stuff?"

"Oh, leave her alone. She's a scarecat," said Koskoris, mockingly. "We don't need any cowards in our Legion."

At that Myrto bent down and wriggled into the hole.

"Take your time looking around," the leader said. "We'll close up the hole now. We'll be back later to get you."

They rolled the stones back into place behind her, and Myrto found herself sealed up in the darkness. She turned on the flashlight and stood there.

"It may be a feat, but it looks a lot like stealing," she said to herself. "And with a flashlight, of course——" She groped until she found the electric light switch. When she turned it on the birds in the shop woke up and began to flutter uneasily in their cages.

"I wonder where the whistles with the white lanyards could be?" Myrto asked herself. She cast an exploratory glance along the shelves. Of course, they would also give her a whistle to hang from her shoulder. And when it became compulsory for everybody in school to be a Legionnaire, she would be a leader; and in the parades she would be first in the line of march, and every now and then she would wheel around and blow the whistle at her Legion.

But what would Mrs. Angeliki say in the morning when she found the things gone? Surely the leader would go to her and say, "I sent my Legionnaire to take them because she had to perform a feat." But supposing he didn't say anything? She wondered if she oughtn't to go out again and ask the leader and Koskoris. But wouldn't they call her a coward then, if they saw her emerge from the hole without the stuff? And then—good-by, Legion! She would never be a leader then.

A noise, like the creaking of a door, made Myrto turn her head in terror.

I didn't have to listen to the rest of the story. I could imagine for myself what happened. Appearing before her, in the little doorway that led into the tiny room with the empty cages, was Niko.

I could just imagine how astonished Myrto had been.

And how astonished Niko had been, too, seeing her there in the locked shop, at night, with a flashlight in her hand. He would have explained to her afterward, of course, that it really was stealing and not a feat.

And Myrto began to cry so hard that Niko was worried about her. After a while he persuaded her to run home quickly, before the others returned. He unlocked the door for her to leave that way. And he gave her his word that he would come to the house to see her and that he himself would tell us what had happened. Only then did Myrto leave off crying long enough to run home.

When Niko finished telling all this, he told Stamatina to go with him to wake Grandfather so that he could say good-by to him.

Then he put his arms around us both and, big as he was, Niko's eyes had tears in them.

"How will you go?" I asked him. "Won't they catch you if they see you on the ship?"

He grinned at me. "I'll ride on the wildcat's back," he said.

"But the wildcat died. Didn't you know?"

"He didn't die, Melissa. He was only wounded. Now he's all well again."

He kissed us once more.

"I'll write to you," he said in a choked whisper. And he followed Stamatina out of our room.

"Come into my bed," Myrto said. "I can't sleep alone."

I crept in beside her.

"Ev-po? Li-po?" I asked her.

"I don't know, Melia."

"I'm ev-po, ev-po! Because the wildcat is still alive!"

⊒ 5 ⊒

The Canary and Spain. Stars and Crabs.
If I Had Been Born a Writer. . .

⊒ When I woke up the next morning, it seemed to me that I had seen it all in a dream. Myrto was still asleep. We had fallen asleep and no one had awakened us. It would be too late to go to school now.

The door opened noiselessly. Mama came in on tip-toes.

"Melia," she said in a whisper so as not to awaken Myrto, "don't go to school today either. Stay home and keep your sister company."

"So you know?" I asked.

"Yes. Stamatina told us everything."

"What's going to happen now, Mama?"

"What's going to happen, Melia?"

"Well, about Myrto and about the Legionnaires? About school?"

"I don't know, Melia. We'll have to think about it."

It seemed so strange to me for Myrto to be in bed. She

hardly ever was sick. Now she just stayed there, lying back and staring at the ceiling. She didn't even want to eat. Great-aunt Despina opened her cupboard and brought out a pile of sweets, but Myrto didn't touch them. I sat beside her. I told her jokes. But nothing helped. She wouldn't even smile. Suddenly she got up from the bed and put on her slippers.

"Do you want something?" I asked.

"I want to go and tell Grandfather and Mama something."

"Wait here. I'll call them."

"No. I'll go downstairs."

I went with her. We burst into the dining room where they were all gathered. Even Papa was there. He hadn't gone to the bank.

"I'm never going back to that rotten school!" Myrto said. "Not even if I never learn anything, not even if I become an illiterate, a piece of unplaned wood, as Grandfather says!"

She turned even paler. I was afraid she was going to faint. Mama took her in her arms. And Grandfather said, "Calm yourself, Myrtoula. You will not go back to that rotten school, as you call it. We'll get a certificate from the doctor saying you are ill, and you'll have your lessons at home with me."

"Then I'll have lessons with you, too," I cried happily. "And so will Alexis!"

"No, Melissa," Grandfather said gravely. "You must finish your year there, so that Mr. Karanasis won't make any trouble for your father. And next year all of you, Alexis, too, will go to the public school. Even if there are a hundred children in every classroom, it won't matter. I'll help you with your lessons. If it becomes compulsory for you to be Legionnaires, and there's no way out of it, why then you'll join. But in your hearts you won't really be Legionnaires."

Then Grandfather smiled and looked at us cheerfully, as though nothing had happened.

"Just pray for a sunny day on Sunday. We'll take Alexis with us and we'll rent a motorboat and go to Lamagari. We'll spend the whole day there."

"Stamatina," Myrto said abruptly, "please give me the eggs I didn't eat this morning." And everybody laughed.

Five days had passed since all that happened and since Niko had left for good. I went to Mrs. Angeliki's to buy a toy "all gold" wristwatch as a present for Artemis, in case we went to Lamagari. Did Mrs. Angeliki know about Myrto's feat, I wondered?

As soon as she caught sight of me she smiled and said, "Wait!"

She climbed onto a chair and, from the middle hook, took down a cage with a canary in it. It was bright yellow, with a single black spot on its head.

"It's yours," she told me. "Yours and Myrto's."

I didn't know what to say. I didn't even dare to stretch out my hand to take it.

"Take it!" she insisted. Then, lowering her voice until it was nearly a whisper, she said, "Niko left it as a present for you."

I walked along the narrow cobbled streets with a big green cage in which the canary fluttered fearfully.

"Don't be frightened," I told it. "Don't be frightened. You'll soon get to know us, and you'll be 'ev-po, ev-po' with us. I'll find you a name, a beautiful name. We'll talk to you about Niko, since you know him too, and about the wildcat. Do you see how hard it is not to walk on the cracks when I hold your cage? But I won't walk on them! And you have to make the wish: may Niko arrive safely, riding on the wildcat!"

As soon as Stamatina saw me with the cage in my hands, she called Myrto, saying we were to wait in the glass-enclosed porch and she would bring us a hook to hang it on. You'd almost think she had been expecting me to bring home the canary.

"Now, instead of the wildcat, we'll have the canary," Myrto said.

"Do you think it might bring us a message from Niko?"

This time, however, it was Stamatina who brought us the message. She dug into her pocket and produced a letter.

"Read it," she said. "Then give it back to me so I can burn it."

It was from Niko.

"Dear young cousins," he wrote. "I have mounted the wildcat's back and I am on my way to Spain. I told you, remember, that they are fighting there. I am going to fight on the side of the men who are singing. One day I'll come back and we will go once again to our Lamagari, the most beautiful spot on earth, and I'll tell you about all our marvelous adventures, the wildcat's and mine. We will fight for Democracy. We will win. And we will bring it to our island. Then both the wildcat's eyes will be blue, bright blue. And Manoli will go to school then and become a musician. Remember, always love the children of Lamagari! And now, farewell. And stay well!"

"Couldn't we call the canary *Iberia?*" I wondered. "Niko says that's another word for Spain."

"Stuff and nonsense!" said Myrto. "That's not a bird's name!"

It was Sunday, and our prayers had been answered, because the sun was shining. Grandfather had kept his promise to take us to Lamagari. The sea was as smooth as oil. You would have thought it was midsummer. I was happy that Alexis would get to know Lamagari. Just imagine, it was so close to the town and he had never gone there, to the most beautiful place in the whole world!

But Alexis had never gone to the country in the summer. His father would arrive from Athens and they would remain in the town. This year, Grandfather said, we would take him to Lamagari for the whole summer while his mother went off to that remote island to see his father.

"But it's such a responsibility, having a boy in the house!" exclaimed Great-aunt Despina in alarm when she heard that Grandfather had invited Alexis.

"You're talking foolishness, Despina!" Grandfather told her for the third time since the dictatorship came.

In the motorboat we felt as though we were flying to

173

Lamagari. And even before we leaped out onto the old sea wall, we started shouting. "Manooooooooli! Arteeeeee-mis! Odysseeeeeus! Auroooooora!"

From the pine trees, from the rocks, from the beach, our friends were already racing toward us.

"That bashful boy, over there, who's he?" Artemis asked, laughing, when she caught sight of Alexis standing a little distance away.

"He's our best friend in the town," I told her.

"Do you still have boarders?" Grandfather asked Manoli.

"The police came and took them away," he said mournfully. "They took them to another island."

"And you, why didn't you come for your lessons?" Grandfather asked in a mock-scolding voice. "We had so many sunny days."

"I found a job in the next village, washing down the horses at the barracks."

"Then we'll have to get some lessons in this summer," Grandfather said, patting his head. Then Grandfather went off to look for Antoni.

Manoli kept tugging at me. He wanted to learn about Niko.

"He went away," I whispered. "We'll tell you later, so that the children can hear about it."

We started running all over Lamagari. How different it was in winter! The castles and the warehouses were locked tight and the shacks seemed even poorer. Only the pebbles, washed over and over again by gales and rainstorms, glittered in the sunshine at the beach's edge.

Down by the shore, abandoned, we came across the *Arion*, Pipitsa's barrel. There was no bottom to it any more. All the iron hoops had been knocked out of place. It reminded us of the Big Pest.

"May I kiss my dead mother and father . . . May they gather me up in tiny little pieces in a basket," Artemis said, mimicking her and setting us all to laughing.

We went to our rocks. I told Manoli, "You have to sit in the throne. You're the oldest now."

Manoli went and sat there. No one spoke. Everything was so quiet that you could hear the ticky-tack of Niko's watch that Manoli wore on his wrist. And we uncovered a nest of crabs. We lifted up some rocks, and a big crab with its little ones began to scurry about like mad, with their funny sideways crawl. Myrto held something up in her palm. She opened her fingers and a faint *plop!* could be heard in the water. Three gold stars shone on the sea floor, beside the colored pebbles. Artemis made a grab for them.

"No!" Myrto cried, and Artemis drew back.

The big crab re-emerged, clamped its claws around a star and lugged it off to its nest. The little crabs tried to drag off the other stars in their claws.

"Oh, they're taking the two that are left!" Artemis cried. "Such lovely shiny stars!"

"They're revolting," Myrto told her. "Leave them alone. I want the crabs to hide them good and deep so that nobody will ever see them again."

"Let's go to the half-armed windmill," Manoli suggested. And we all started racing in that direction.

We gave the half-open door a shove. It creaked again, just as it had last summer. The twisting staircase came into sight. But there were no footsteps to be heard, and Niko did not appear, smiling, before us. We climbed up to his little room. A jug, half full of water, stood in a corner, forgotten.

Then Myrto and I told the others the news. "Niko has gone to Spain!"

And we told them about his letter, which we had learned by heart.

If I had been born a writer, I would write a very happy story. I would write about Niko and the wildcat. But I would not write about Niko's hiding in the windmill with the half-arm and in the tiny room with the bird cages. Nor would I write about how the wildcat fell wounded in the parlor. I would write about Niko's returning, riding on the wildcat's back, both its eyes having now turned sky-blue. They might even fly back, having discovered how men and wildcats can fly. First of all they would come back to us, at Lamagari. Then they would fly to all the countries of the world. And wherever they went, they would make all the children "ev-po, ev-po!"

"Which way is Spain?" Odysseus asked when we were sitting on a rock trying to catch our breath after all that crazy running.

"Over there," said Myrto, pointing somewhere out to sea.

Then—you would think we had agreed to do it ahead of time—we all stood on top of the rocks and cupped our hands and called:

"Stay well, Nikoooo! Can you hear us? Stay well, Nikoooo!"

The wind bore our voices far away over the sea. Alexis called too, even though he had never known Niko and the wildcat in the glass case.

When she was ten Alki Zei decided to be a writer, but her career was not begun in earnest until she went to high school, where she wrote plays for the school stage and for the puppet theatre in which she acted as well. After their marriage, she and her husband, a writer and stage director, left Greece for long sojourns in Uzbekistan, Italy, France, and Russia. While they were in Moscow her two children were born and she studied scenario writing at the Moscow Institute of Cinema; she also wrote several stories and her first book, *Wildcat Under Glass*. Although she had been long away from Greece when she wrote it, the inspiration for the book was drawn from the country where she was born and grew up, and its setting and incidents come from her Greek childhood and life under the Fascist dictatorship in Greece which she experienced as a young girl. She and her family returned later to Greece but moved to Paris after the dictatorship of April 21, 1967 took control of Greece.

A noted author in his own right, Edward Fenton has written over fifteen books for children and adults. He was born in New York and studied at Amherst College but then lived abroad in Italy and in Greece for long periods. There he became fluent in their languages, acquired a feeling for the people and the country based on living there, and found the background for some of his books for young readers: from Italy, *A Matter of Miracles* and *The Golden Doors;* and from Greece, *Aleko's Island* and *An Island for a Pelican*. While he was in Greece he read *Wildcat Under Glass* in Greek, was very taken with the book, and arranged to meet the author. They became good friends and it was a natural step for Mr. Fenton to undertake the English translation of the book. In Greece, also, he met and married a distinguished Greek child psychologist. The Fentons now have returned to the United States where they live in Washington, D.C.